The Gates of Hell

The Gates of Hell

by
Maurice Level

Translated, annotated and introduced by
Jessica Sequeira

A Black Coat Press Book

ISBN 978-1-61227-598-7. First Printing. February 2017. Published by Black Coat Press, an imprint of Hollywood Comics.com, LLC, P.O. Box 17270, Encino, CA 91416.

TABLE OF CONTENTS

Introduction

La porte de l'enfer, the enormous bronze sculpture by Auguste Rodin, was commissioned in 1880 and delivered to the French Directorate of Fine Arts in 1917. These "gates of hell" depict scenes from the Inferno section of Dante's Divine Comedy, from the Thinker to the Kiss to the Three Shades to the Eternal Springtime, assembling a cast of over two hundred carefully formed figures. Maurice Level's collection of stories *Les portes de l'enfer*, published as a collection in 1910 but written over the course of decades, possibly has a direct link to Rodin's famous work. The world of Parisian writers and artists during the period was quite small, and it is very likely that Level (1875-1926) traveled in the same circles as the sculptor, his contemporary. After working briefly as a doctor, Level dedicated himself to writing for newspapers and theater, and also became involved in the art world. Along with his brothers Émile, Jacques and André, he organized the association La Peau de l'Ours from 1904 to 1914, responsible for the sale of works by Matisse, Denis, Dufy, Gauguin, Picasso, Redon, van Gogh, Bonnard, Vuillard and others. This is a probable point of intersection. More extensive biographical information on Maurice is lacking, and it seems that what we know about the man will have to come primarily from his works. Even if there is not a direct connection to Rodin's *Gates*, however, to look at the sculpture is to recognize the same triumphs and agonies, the same

7

cleanly carved forms and dramatic posturing, as those that appear in Level's tales.

The twenty-six stories in *The Gates of Hell*, which form a part of the *conte cruel* tradition, range in subject matter from a man who keeps a secret with devastating effects, to a maniac who finds thrills in witnessing violent accidents, to a blind man who purposely loses his eyesight, to a prostitute who by chance sleeps with the man who executed her husband. The rich and intricate stories ratchet up suspense sentence by sentence, with a horror based on human behavior and psychological drama rather than supernatural elements. The subtle beauty to be found in their descriptions is only further intensified by the slow, excruciating turn of their knife: a decadent pleasure. The macabre tales have been compared to those of Level's cousin Marcel Schwob, as well as those of Villiers de l'Isle-Adam, Octave Mirbeau, Jules Barbey d'Aurevilly, Guy de Maupassant and Edgar Allen Poe. They were printed in Parisian newspapers of the period and later adapted to the stage, according to rumors with the help of Level's wife. This was not just any stage, but the famous Théâtre du Grand-Guignol, the enormously popular Theatre of Horrors of the period, located in the Pigalle area of Paris.

What characterizes Level's *contes cruels*? The French tradition of fear and the macabre relied on realism, rather than the mystical or supernatural, for its effects. The horror in Level's stories comes from the fact that despite their improbable events or unlikely locations (a house being robbed, a prison cell, the top of a speeding train) everything that occurs could indeed really have happened. This is a dark realism with no need of castles, witches' circles or macabre beasts. In his 1925 essay

"Supernatural Horror in Literature", HP Lovecraft writes:

Villiers de l'Isle-Adam [...] followed the macabre school; his "Torture by Hope", the tale of a stake-condemned prisoner permitted to escape in order to feel the pangs of recapture, is held by some to constitute the most harrowing short story in literature. This type, however, is less a part of the weird tradition than a class peculiar to itself—the so-called conte cruel, *in which the wrenching of the emotions is accomplished through dramatic tantalizations, frustrations, and gruesome physical horrors. Almost wholly devoted to this form is the living writer Maurice Level, whose very brief episodes have lent themselves so readily to theatrical adaptation in the "thrillers" of the Grand Guignol. As a matter of fact, the French genius is more naturally suited to this dark realism than to the suggestion of the unseen; since the latter process requires, for its best and most sympathetic development on a large scale, the inherent mysticism of the Northern mind.*

Level's style is tremendously economical, and each action or quote is charged with meaning. All events are triggered by something, without loose description. Nothing just happens, and there is no idle chatter; every action and conversation has a purpose and creates an effect. The mind operates in a similar way; the mechanism of the psyche is wound up and allowed to run. People left alone with themselves are thus not to be trusted, as in their minds a small thing such as the crow of a rooster is capable of amplifying into something much larger, distorted into grandiose and tragic proportions. In anxious or simple people especially, a throwaway phrase such as "mitigating circumstances" can have the most disastrous effects. Even an intelligent and perfectly sane person can be driven in conditions of extreme stress to madness, which always results in an action.

The unease and disquiet that Level's work entails requires a very close attention to detail, small spaces and confined interiors, as unease only works in an area so cramped one finds it hard to breathe. So, for instance, a prison is the perfect environment for terror, or the inside of a well, or the top of a train, or the basement room of an empty house. Phrases crystallize with similarly luminous intensity, just like chinks of light in the darkness or mirror shards. Clocks play an important role, especially clocks that have stopped or have no hands, and less literally each story is also a tiny and bejeweled mechanical watch set to tick. At precisely the right moment, the stiff's mouth will spring open and the fly will come buzzing out.

Objects have a special power; a mirror shard or gun can be the trigger for the tight descending convolutions of the mind, the inverse of an icon or the photograph of a loved one long contemplated, which raises one to a state of calm and grace. This is a bourgeois world of interiors and exquisite things, pearl-handled knives and silver cutlery, co-existing with another world of prostitutes and beggars looking for a warm crust of bread. There is an exquisite gleaming "selfness" to each object, word or sensation, just like the sound of a metal shovel scooping up earth. Things and actions are clearly delineated, and the only cloudiness that appears is in the mind: or rather, not cloudiness, just false logic, prompted by attachment. Disproportional angst can give rise to situational comedy, such as a frightened thief violently and repeatedly stabbing the body of a man already dead. Far from opposites, the intense and the darkly humorous can easily co-exist, spurring themselves and the plot onward.

Terror, in Level's stories, is set in motion by something external, but it is the aloneness of a person with his or her own thoughts that amplifies a guilt-provoking action, everyday object, forbidden desire or simple anxiety into terror. The transition from stasis to white-hot energy and action is not sudden but proceeds gradually. For while madness and terror come from within, they are the response to terrors without. The madman or madwoman is not to be emulated or pitied, but rather seen as the victim of a machine set in motion by something outside herself, with a devastating effect on her nerves. A certain preliminary atmosphere permits this to occur. Half-light and half-open doors appear everywhere, and ellipses permeate the dialogue; these extend into the internal monologues of the mind, as if the normal condition were one of uncertainty, incompleteness or hesitation, and madness only an extension of this. This hesitation afflicts even supposed professionals such as doctors, who are nervy and trembling on the job rather than sources of healing and authority. In this field of hesitation, the seed of doubt is easily planted.

Small inflicted cruelties, such as depriving an imprisoned man of his favorite shard of glass, can have immense consequences. Where do such cruelties come from? Circumstances, animals, nature, other people. Circumstance is cruel in that things happen mercilessly and "just because", such as the prostitute My Eye's happening to sleep with her husband's executioner. Animals are cruel in that, like the toad in one of the tales, they can be perverse and willful, seeking revenge. Nature is cruel in that it is less mysterious than apathetic; the waters of the Seine can close over a body coldly and dispassionately.

It is only mysterious in the sense that it is something incapable of being understood and with no secret to impart, something that defies comprehension in its very superficiality. In Level's world, there is nothing supernatural, and flat surfaces are what most terrify. With nothing divine, with no authority figure one can trust, everything turns into a kind of theater. The stability of reality is paper-thin, easily threatened by a chance encounter. Other people are thus another kind of cruelty, especially those who don't mean to be cruel, but are simply interested in pursuing their own ends. Evil is not perversity but the rational pursuits of the ego with no regard for consequences or the feelings of others. (The reverse is also true: goodness is disinterested joy in helping someone else, feeling oneself loved without wanting anything in return.)

There is an additional source of unintentional cruelty: the stripping away of illusion. The question of what is reality and what is illusion appears over and over again in *The Gates of Hell*. In the relationships in the stories, whether romantic, between friends or between parent-child, the "real" is often sacrificed to preserve a happy illusion or avoid pain. In one story, a mother lies on behalf of her child in court, so that she can continue to believe he is a good boy. In another, a man who regains his vision deliberately blinds himself again, so as not to have to accept seeing the consequences of his wife's affair. In a third, a woman lies to her husband, telling him over and over again that morning hasn't come, rather than give him the terrible news there is darkness because he's gone blind. False kindnesses, the illusion of a reality masked in courtesies, are another kind of playacting.

When one cannot rely on those one loves to be brutally honest, encounters with strangers are always potentially destabilizing, since the truth might come out. Here, again, the tension between outer and inner emerges. Is there such a thing as an inner reality of events, or is truth the same thing as its representation? The symbolists believed that every object and word has a meaning behind it, but the decadent writers who followed them took a more cynical view; for them all reality is the same as its stage set. It is significant that although these pieces were performed onstage at the Grand Guignol, they began as stories, for the psychological detail they accrue surpasses what can be acted out in physical gestures. This is the tragedy of the theater: even the most complex psychological subtleties must be depicted through movement of the body, props and sets. In the tales of Level, a sensitive writer who also knew how to entertain his rowdy audiences, this tension between theatrical outer events and inner understanding proved to be fertile territory, for it drew on the real philosophical source of terror: the possibility of meaninglessness. How will human beings behave if those gates lead onto nothing?

Jessica Sequeira

Sources

100 Wild Little Weird Tales, ed. Stefan R. Dziemianowicz, Martin H. Greenberg and Robert Weinberg

The Grand Guignol: theatre of fear and terror, ed. Mel Gordon

Grand-Guignol: the French theatre of horror, Richard J. Hand and Michael Wilson

Searchers after horror: new tales of the weird and fantastic, S T Joshi

Supernatural Horror in Literature, HP Lovecraft

Le roman symboliste: un art de l'extrême conscience: Edouard Dujardin, André Gide, Remy de Gourmont and Marcel Schwob, Valérie Michelet Jacquod

Historical dictionary of fantasy literature, Brian Stableford

La chair du livre: matérialité, imaginaire et poétique du livre fin-de-siècle, Evanghélia Stead

The Symbolist Movement in Literature, Arthur Symons

Fantastic French fiction of mystery and emotion, ed. James Burton Tharp

Under the Red Light

Sitting in a large armchair beside the fire, elbows on his knees and hands stretched toward the flames, speaking in a slow voice, he abruptly began to whisper: "Yes… yes…," as if he needed to acknowledge his recollections and verify his weary memory before taking up his interrupted thoughts once more.

On the table lay papers, books, a handkerchief. The lamp gave out a poor light, so that I could see nothing of him but his slightly gray face and his hands that in the light from the hearth cast two long shadows.

The purr of the cat in front of the fire, and the crackling of logs on which strange gleams danced, were all that disturbed the silence. His voice seemed to come from very far off, as if he were dreaming:

"Yes… yes… It was the great, the very greatest misfortune of my life. I could stand being reduced to poverty, being crippled… anything… but not that! To have lived ten years beside a beloved wife, to see her disappear and to remain alone, all alone, with the lonely future ahead… That's not easy!… Soon it will be six months since she's gone!… how long it's been! and how brief the time before that!… Even if it's true I'd been ill for a while, if only she'd helped me understand!… It's terrible to say, but when you know in advance, your reason can prepare itself… the heart empties little by little, and you get used to it… but like this!…"

"I thought," I said, "that she'd been suffering for some time?"

He nodded:

"Everything, everything went wrong... The doctors could never say what was wrong with her... She was taken from me in two days. How or why I've lived since then, I don't know. I pace through the house all day long, chasing a fleeing memory, imagining that she'll step out from behind a curtain, that a bit of her scent still floats through these empty rooms..."

He stretched out his hand across the table:

"Yesterday, I found this, look... this veil was in one of my pockets. She'd given it to me one evening when we were going to the theater. It still seems to smell of her perfume, still seems warm from having brushed her face... but no! Everything is gone: only sorrow remains... Anything else would have been fine, but this!...

In the first moments of pain, extraordinary ideas can occur to you... Would you believe that I photographed her on her deathbed! In that poor bedroom her soul had just departed, I set up my camera and lit the magnesium; at that dreadful moment, I prepared, carefully and with meticulous precaution, things that today repel me... Even so, when I think of that photo, I tell myself she's there, that I can see her just as I saw her the last time!"

"And where do you keep the portrait?" I asked him.

He leaned forward a little, and replied softly:

"I don't have it, or rather, I do... on film. But I've never had the courage to develop it... it remains in the camera... I'm afraid of touching it... and yet! How I'd like to!..."

He put his hand on my arm:

"Listen: tonight... with you here... speaking with you... I feel better... I feel strong... Will you come with me to my laboratory... Shall we develop the film?..."

He searched my face with the anxious look of a child who trembles at the thought of being denied his desired toy.

"Alright," I said.

He rose quickly.

"Yes… With you, it won't be the same… With you, I'll be calmer… and this will do me good… a great deal of good… you'll see…"

We entered his laboratory: a darkroom in which bottles were arranged on the shelves. A slab with a basin, vials and books stretched from one wall to the other.

He didn't speak, checking labels on bottles and wiping vials, as the trembling candlelight cast quivering shadows around him.

After lighting a red glass lantern, he put out the candle and said:

"Close the door."

That darkness, cut through by bloody light, had something dramatic about it. Unsettling reflections clung to the sides of bottles, to the wrinkles on his cheeks, to his hollow temples.

He said:

"Is the door closed? Then I'll begin."

He opened the chamber of the camera and removed the plate. He picked it up carefully, fingers spread, thumbs and index grasping the corners, and stared a long time, as if his eyes could see the sleeping image that would soon awaken.

He murmured:

"There she is! It's horrible!…"

Then he slowly let it slip into the bath, and began to stir the basin.

I don't know why, but the sound of the enamel tongs hitting the basin at regular intervals seemed to me strange and painful. Under the red light, the liquid splashed against the plate in a monotonous back-and-forth motion: the faint noise it made reminded me of the sound of sobbing, and I couldn't take my eyes off the square of milky-colored glass, which little by little was being tinted black at the edges.

Clear at first, the bath darkened gradually; and soon, a smudge appeared in the middle of the plate, which gradually widened, softening in areas into a lighter shade.

I looked at my friend. His trembling lips murmured unintelligible words.

He removed the plate, lifted it to the level of his eyes, and spoke, as I peered over his shoulder:

"Now it's coming... slowly... my bath is so weak... but that doesn't matter... The whites are appearing... Just wait... you'll see..."

He dropped the plate, which sank into the liquid with a suction-like noise.

There it appeared a uniform gray color. He lowered his head and said simply:

"That black rectangle is the bed... Above it, this square you see (he pointed it out with a flick of his chin) is the pillow; and in the middle, this lighter zone with a pale stripe that contrasts with the black background... that's her... with the crucifix I placed between her fingers."

His voice choked a little:

"My poor thing... my darling!..."

Tears ran down his cheeks, he gave out painful hiccups... He wept, effortlessly, like those in the habit of sorrow, for whom crying has become as familiar as smiling.

Through tears, he said:

"The details are growing clearer... Here, near her, are lighted candles and a branch of blessed box elder... here is her hair I loved so much... her hands she was so proud of... and the little white rosary she kept in a prayer book... my God!... It hurts me to see all this again, and yet I am happy... very happy... It seems that I'm looking at her, my poor little one..."

Feeling that emotion was overcoming him, I wanted to hurry things along. I said:

"Don't you think the plate has been in long enough...?"

He removed the plate, approached the lantern, examined it closely, put it in the bath again, took it out again, examined it once more and whispered:

"No... no..."

I remember that the sound of his voice and abruptness of his gesture struck me. But I had no time to think, for he began to speak again.

"There are things that still need to come out... It will take a while, but I told you... my bath is weak... the details only appear gradually."

He counted: One... two... three... four... five...

"Now it's been long enough. I wouldn't like to keep it in too long, and damage it..."

He picked up the plate again, shook it up and down, rinsed it in water and handed it to me:

"Look."

But suddenly, as I held out my hand, he drew back rapidly, leaned over and held the film to the light. At that moment his face lit by the red light seemed so frightening that I cried out:

"What's wrong?"

His eyes were open too wide, his raised lips exposed his teeth, his jaws chattered; I could hear his heart leap in his chest, and saw his big body sway back and forth.

I put my hand on his shoulder, trying to understand what had provoked that dreadful anguish. For the second time I cried out:

"Well… answer me… what's the matter?"

Then, turning a face toward me with nothing human left in it, sinking his bloodshot eyes in mine, he grabbed my wrist with such a brutal movement that his nails dug into my flesh.

Three times he opened his mouth, attempting to speak, and then waved the film above his head, screaming into the night flecked with red:

"The matter!… The matter!… Wretch! Scoundrel! Assassin that I am! The matter… she wasn't dead!… The matter… Her eyes moved!…"

Sun

Because he was picked up on a winter evening, a wailing little thing near a railway station; because nothing in his babble indicated the initial of any name; and because misfortunate children are the ones the Lord loves most and lays claim to, he was called Paradieu.

Until he was twelve years old, he stayed at a children's shelter. Then one fine day he fled and took to the road, a bag on his back and a stick in his hand.

From that time on, he lived haphazardly, partly from charity, partly from work in the countryside. He never remained in the same place for too long, perhaps in the fear that his location would be discovered, or perhaps simply guided by a vague instinct that pushed him toward the wide horizon, the fields of summer wheat, the great woods that sing their eternal song with melodies and words only comprehensible to those who fall asleep in their shadow.

He became a man. One morning policemen woke him at the edge of a ditch and arrested him for vagrancy. They asked him some quick questions and learned he belonged to a departing regiment. He'd been declared missing and had to be back at the barracks in a few days.

"You're lucky to have been discovered like this!" they said. "One week later and you'd have been arrested for disobedience."

He didn't know how exactly he'd been lucky, or what the word "disobedience" meant. But because he was gentle and shy, he smiled.

"Yes, I'm lucky!"

He let himself be taken to the base without rebellion or regret.

At first, life seemed easy and gentle. He was used to sleeping most nights under the stars, eating only when he got lucky on the road, shivering in winter under rags filled with holes and walking all day with an empty stomach and weak legs. Looking at the autumn sky, the bare earth, the leafless and glowing trees, he thought that when they'd spoken of his luck, they meant his current period of rest, so different from his past of poverty... He was surprised to hear his comrades complain, but he spoke little, knowing very few words.

Winter was harsh. Every day, once exercises were over, he would contemplate the roofs blanketed with snow, the birds in the gutters that tapped the ice to slake their thirst, the chimneys from which a light smoke drifted up, and thought:

"I'm safe now!... I have a bed!... In the barracks, the stove is humming... I'm well!..."

But as soon as the first buds bloomed at the tips of the branches with the return of spring, as soon as he saw the sun again, the clear sky and bright mornings, a strange restlessness took hold of him.

Leaning out the window, fists under his chin, ears filled with a vague rustling, eyes half-closed, he forgot the shelter during cold weather and the warm clothing. With his mouth wide open, he breathed in deeply. The breeze had in it the perfume of the countryside, the immensity of wide-open spaces, the memory of his freedom in rags...

He grew sad, worried, nervous. One evening after supper, he fled, racing across the fields. But no matter how far he ran, he still smelled the breath of the city, saw the blue roofs of the houses and tall chimneys of the factories and heard the ringing of bells in the barracks, which prevented him from enjoying the vast horizons and music of the plains... He spoke to himself:

"You aren't made for that life!... You must take up your stick again, your knapsack!... Yes... but... and the prison...?"

And so he returned.

He resisted with all his strength for another two weeks. He was so sad, so tired, that his comrades said to him:

"You must report sick, Paradieu!"

But he shook his head, and one fine evening, he was no longer there. Just as usual he had gone out at five, then stolen an old pair of trousers and coat from a secondhand shop, thrown his uniform and bayonet over the bridge and failed to report to his barracks.

All night and all day he went on walking. Drunkenness had taken hold of him. He went on under the deep blue sky, free, joyful, headed for adventure. In the shade of the willows, sitting beside a stream, he laughed and cried at the same time, hands clasped in ecstasy before the clear water, looking out at the flight of the dragonflies, the waving of the grass and the green blanket of the fields, where beasts contentedly grazed.

Yet the carefreeness of the old times was no longer in him. His brief contact with ordinary men had given him the notion, dark and threatening, of punishment.

Of course he still loved the woods and large meadows, the trees that wept and the springs that sang. He loved them perhaps more than he had ever loved them, and the sun too, that giant companion that made the days radiant and warmed the nights. He loved them... but was terrified of their being torn away from him. He did not dare pass through the villages anymore, as now he feared men and fled from them.

Then, at the bend of a path, there were suddenly policemen grabbing his collar.

Brought before a military tribunal, he was charged with desertion and destruction of military effects, and sentenced to five years in prison.

He did not truly understand the horror — not his wrongdoing, but his punishment — until he arrived in the police car at the jail.

He put on the trousers and brown jacket, and the cap with its long visor, in a small courtyard surrounded by white walls, so high he had to throw his head back to see the sky. Standing there in front of the dark bunkers and skeletal trees, a deadly chill ran down the back of his neck. He tried to reason with himself a little:

"I'm not entirely lost, since I still see the sky... as long as you see the sun and sky, there's hope... otherwise this would be death..."

But after twenty-four hours, he began to suffer horribly. At the barracks, he had been almost free. Once the day was over, he could gallop through the fields. During the exercises at the ramparts, his feet had treaded green grass, and in front of him he could see what had once been his: Space!...

While here, he had to stay all day in the workshop, under the evil eye of the military officer...

He became aggressive and evasive. At last understanding his impotence, he opposed everything with the force of inertia, unable to stifle the rebellion of his heart.

He had to remain an apprentice for three months. At the end of that time, he was put to work. He said:

"I don't know..."

"If your task isn't done, and done well, by tomorrow you'll have four more days in the cell..."

He replied calmly:

"It's likely it won't be done."

"Well then, off you go then!"

They pushed him into the cell. He heard the door close once again on him, and the keys turn in the locks. There he remained, alone in total darkness. He tore out his hair...

Ah! Those scoundrels! From the start they'd found for him the worst possible torture! He, for whom light was life, had been thrown into darkness! They'd torn away the sun little by little... A little at the barracks to begin with... then, at the prison... Then, in the bunkers... And then finally, since a little still remained to him, a very tiny bit, just enough so as not to die... They'd taken that from him too..."

Yet when he opened his eyes wide, he noticed that a little light had slipped between the sealed bars above the door. He followed the beam. It seemed to come from down the hall... then was lost. He paced in his cell, trying to orient himself, reflecting:

"If the light makes it here, the sky must not be far. Yes... But, to see it!... To see the sky... Just the slightest bit... A little wedge... So tiny..."

He put his hands in his pockets and felt something smooth, a piece of mirror that he'd picked up in the courtyard not long before. He took it in his hand, and the mirror seemed to glow. He thought:

"Well?... what does this mean?..."

He realized he was directly in the path of the beam of light. And suddenly, sitting on his bunk, still staring at the mirror, he let out a cry.

In his hand, in the depths of the square of glass, a scrap of sky could be seen: just a scrap, but blue, clear and so bright it seemed a dancing star at the bottom of a well.

His distress burst into an immense joy. He dared not make a move, fearing the dear image would flee, and little by little a strange thought came into his mind:

Wasn't he better off here than at the workshop? Was he cold?… Was it dark?… No! since he had the sky!… At least he was alone… He could think, cry or laugh as he liked, without the fierce glare of the sergeant major weighing on him. Comparing the two prisons, he preferred this one. There was only one thing to do: Stay.

From then on, to be punished in the cell, he learned to be cunning, calculating to the last penny the price of his misdeeds, rubbing his hands together as soon as an extension in his time was announced. He behaved poorly, sure of not being found out.

When he had spent 120 days locked up — for in the jails, the length of time in a cell has no limit but the resistance of a man — he began to breathe more calmly.

The patch of sky in the palm of his hand was enough to make him dream. Immediately when he woke, he turned to look at it, and said:

"Such beautiful weather today."

Or:

"Bad weather!… We'll have rain…"

His imagination became keener every day, and he lived for himself alone, an intense and profound life. If by chance, the wing of a bird streaked a brown arrow through his sky, he believed he could see all the nests of the forest, and hear the warbles from thousands of beaks echoing through the branches.

One morning, while deep in his contemplation, the military officer opened his cell and called to him:

"Come here, Paradieu!"

Lost in his dream, Paradieu didn't answer.

"Hey! Are you deaf?… Come on, outside!"

He didn't move. The officer shook him by the sleeve:

"Do I have to drag you out?"

As he was very weak, he let himself be taken without resistance, but the light dazzled him, and he started to shake.

"Are you unable to move anymore?…"

He leaned against the wall to keep from falling, trying to hide his piece of mirror.

"What are you hiding there?"

He stammered:

"Nothing… Nothing…"

The officer pried open his fingers, and seeing the tiny mirror, sneered:

"What's that?"

He looked him directly in the eyes and said:

"My sun!"

"How'd you like it if I slapped 'your sun' in the air!…"

Paradieu closed his hand quickly and backed away toward the wall.

"Come on, come on," growled the officer, "hurry along now!"

With the back of his hand, he then gave a sharp blow to the other's wrist, so sudden that the mirror fell to the ground and broke.

Something terrible crossed over Paradieu's face. His eyes opened, overly wide; he didn't say a word, but took a step forward. Suddenly his hands descended on the neck of the officer, clinging to it so tightly that the skin bled beneath his fingernails and the body fell, rolled about and lay still. Leaning over the purple face, breath-

27

less and foaming at the teeth, he gasped:

"You stole my sun!... You stole it from me... stole..."

Then he knelt down, picked up the remains of the piece of glass with a trembling hand, and began to cry with great silent sobs, just as the elderly and small children do...

Right to the Knife

"Take a seat, doctor, I beg you, and forgive me for having kept you waiting…"

With a shake of his head, the doctor refused the seat offered to him.

He was a small skinny man with thin limbs. He had a very pale face with big tired eyes, and a beard of a pale blond color that in places revealed his thin cheeks, the same sad beard an adolescent or ill man might have. He was dressed entirely in black, that matte black which when worn too much goes white at the elbows and along the seams. In his oversized clothes, he seemed even more slight and sickly, and his hands half-covered by cuffs looked slender and feeble, like those of a child, a frail little girl.

"How may I be at your service?"

In a trembling voice, so low one could hardly hear it, he replied:

"I've come to ask you to arrest me, sir…"

The magistrate opened his mouth to cry out, but the doctor spoke first:

"Yes, I repeat what I said: I've come to ask you to arrest me."

Then, as if these words had suddenly whipped up his courage, with more fluid movements and a more confident voice, he spoke:

"You know that two years ago, I moved to this neighborhood. I believe I have always been an honest and good man. Whenever necessary, I visited and cared for the needy, never bargaining either my time or my efforts. But what you do not know is the exact situation in which I find myself. This is what I must tell you after the way I have approached you, and before my confession.

I was fourteen when my father died. I was left alone with my mother, with no other resource but the few hundred franc notes we could find at home. I had to enter a profession and try right away to learn a trade, to earn a living. My mother wouldn't hear of taking me out of school. So I finished my studies, mechanically, without asking myself about my real skills or tastes. It had been decided that I'd do a degree in medicine, since I am a doctor's son. And so I found myself at twenty-five years old with a diploma in my hands, without a penny in my pocket. It's very nice to have a title... but you must also possess the talent to use it!

Still, I wasn't discouraged. By asking for favors here and there I managed to buy myself some furniture, scraping together enough to pay the rent a little while. I set up in your neighborhood.

I was full of illusions. After six months, these had been knocked away: I'd eaten up the few sous collected with such difficulty, and earned nothing!...

It was then that my mother and I began the horrible existence of those who keep quiet about their misery. There are some trades in which one doesn't have the right to be needy. I lost two or three patients because I sent notice of my fees too early. What do you expect? When for the last two days we'd eaten only bread, when I was trembling as the month ended, and could only think: someone owes you a hundred francs... so I asked for them. But I told myself:

"Have courage. Better days will come."

Ah! But the more this went on, the less I saw of my patients. Sometimes, to give my mother a bigger end of bread, I came back around at two or three in the afternoon, saying I'd had lunch with a friend. And the debts increased... and increased!... Ideas of suicide crossed my mind at times. But even that was too much for me. There were moments I didn't have the six sous needed to buy coal for asphyxiation.

Courage and strength have their limits, and I had exceeded mine, when one night a visitor arrived. Only someone who's been a new doctor can understand my joy at the sound of that ringing doorbell, which made me jump out of bed.

I dressed quickly and went to the patient's bedside. Beside him was his wife, his two children, a maid. All of them were in a panic. He'd been taken suddenly by pains, vomiting and hiccups. I didn't need a very long examination to arrive at my diagnosis: it was appendicitis. I told his wife, and she asked me:

"Does he need an operation?"

The case seemed so violent, so serious, that against the rule usually followed, which advises the doctor to wait until crisis has passed, I replied:

"Yes."

"When?" she pleaded.

"As soon as possible. Tomorrow, first thing."

So far, nothing unlawful in my conduct. But no sooner had I uttered the word "operation" than an idea leaped before my eyes, which wouldn't leave me.

I looked around. The room I hadn't given any attention to until then now seemed elegant, almost luxurious.

It was the first time I'd attended to a rich client since I'd moved to the neighborhood. My first impulse had been to say:

"You must call a surgeon."

But that sentence didn't come from my mouth. Straight away I said to myself:

"Idiot! You're going to profit another with this windfall. You'll let a man you don't even know earn fifty or a hundred louis! He doesn't need it, while you, poor devil, will get ten francs for your night visit, no more than a crumb! Operate on him yourself!"

I struggled for a long time against that imperious voice.

"But I don't know how... I'll kill him... I have no right..."

The voice sneered:

"No right? You were issued a diploma, and what is it doing for you? It's not telling you: I allow you to do this and not that. It gives you carte blanche. You have nothing but your conscience as a referee, and I, your conscience, shout to you: Go! go! it is bread! You have not eaten for two days. Your old mother is dying of hunger. In fifteen days your landlord will throw you both in the street..."

It was this awful voice that spoke through my mouth when I said:

"I will operate on the patient tomorrow morning."

I trembled when saying these words. If the family had raised the slightest objection, I would have declared myself incompetent. Let me go further: I wished they'd asked for someone more experienced, but they said nothing to me. I had inspired confidence in these people... they delivered themselves to me... Back in my office, I took my head in my hands and told myself: This is madness! It's a crime! You hardly know how to dissect, and you're assuming the right to take a knife and operate on the living!... No... No... You won't do that for mon-

32

ey!…

But the evil one was already leaning over my shoulder again, mocking:

"Fool! Coward! Weakling!"

He taunted me that way all night, and by the time morning arrived, he had taken control of my reason once again.

"Eh! Of course! I'd be too stupid, really! I have the right! There's nothing on the parchment granting me the title of Doctor in Medicine that prohibits me from operating! I have the right! I have the right!…"

Feverish, I began to flip through my books, like a lazy student in a rush an hour before the exam. I skimmed pages and pages… the words paraded before my eyes without leaving a trace… The drawings and names of parts passed before my eyes… before my eyes…

At eight o'clock I took the few instruments I hadn't yet pawned or sold: some pliers, two scalpels and retractors. On the way, I stopped by an old classmate's house and begged for him to lend me some chloroform. Then I continued to my clients' house.

During the preparations I regained my composure a bit. I stretched a sheet out in the bedroom and placed an oilcloth on the table. I sterilized my instruments as best I could. But I knew I was dragging all this out at length to delay the decisive moment of the surgical procedure itself. At last I began.

From the first incision, everything went wrong. I grew nervous at an artery that slipped a little, which I couldn't grasp with my pliers. All the things that seem so simple when you see them done by someone else now seemed terribly difficult. I cut. I pinched. I tied, without seeing or knowing just what I was doing. When my hand went into the wound, I lost my head completely. I'm convinced that with composure, I could have carried out the procedure... But remorse, terror at moral responsibility, and fear, hideous fear, overcame me. After an hour of disordered efforts, with my reason adrift, my head on fire and my kidneys burning, my only desire was to save myself and be alone. Without having done anything but make a gaping wound, I closed the patient up, multiplying the stitches as if that would better conceal my crime.

Once the patient was lying in bed, his wife handed me an envelope. It contained ten hundred franc notes. I experienced a second of joy — oh! one second, only one! — for immediately reality crossed into my path, dragging remorse with it. The voice that had spoken in the night was silent. Now I know what that voice was! It wasn't my conscience, like it said. It was a thief, a criminal, who to better slip past me had taken another name and appearance, but was really Poverty, hideous Poverty! Now that it had worked its evil, it leaped over me like an escaped cat, and I was alone.

My patient lived another two days, which for me were two days of torture and terror. Hour after hour, I was forced to follow the progress of my crime. Yes, my crime, for having seen the desperate resistance this man opposed to death, I am certain that with a good operation he would have survived.

When everything was over, those poor people did not have a word of reproach.

If they'd only known!...

But I cannot hold back any longer. I haven't touched those thousand francs. They burn my fingers, I don't want them any more... You understand... Take them... here they are...

No matter how much I tell myself the law can do

nothing against me, that I had the right to operate, I cannot regard myself as anything but a criminal. And those who in five years of studies did not made me anything more than a faith healer and quack, and gave me the right to hide behind a lying diploma, they are criminals too... If there is no law against me and against them, one must be made... I must be arrested... I killed coldly and deliberately... I can no longer live freely with this pain in my heart... Arrest me, sir..."

The Rooster Crowed

"What a surprise this is! said the old woman when she saw me. "It's so lovely to see you again, so wonderful!"

While climbing the steep path bordered by flowering hedges, she looked at me, curious:

"To think it was four years since you left! Oh! you haven't changed; I knew it was you right away... It's the others who will be amazed!

As we'd arrived at the gate, I asked her:

"And your husband, still going strong?"

"My husband?..."

Her voice dropped.

"My husband... you don't know, it's true. For almost two years now he has been blind."

Blind! In the splendor of that August morning, under the dazzling light that came from the quiet sky, filtering down through the trees with their heavy branches and painting tiger-like patterns on the golden fields, the word "blind" sounded strange.

We pushed through the gate into the garden.

"Hello! Husband," cried the old lady, "Tell the little one to help you come down. Here's a visit that will make you happy."

From the house, a sad voice replied:

"Who's that?"

"Mister Jean!"

The old man appeared on the doorstop. He was tall, but bent over; his black hair had turned white, and his calloused hands rested on the shoulder of the child who served as his guide. I went to him. He seemed very moved, and his lips trembled.

"You'll have lunch with us, won't you?"

"With pleasure."

"Wife, what good things will you give him, the Parisian?"

"Ah! she said, "if only you'd come on Saturday, then we'd have had a choice. Now we'll have to be happy with what we have. First we'll make you an omelet with ham, then we'll twist the neck of a chicken and pick some beautiful artichokes. For dessert, fruit and cream. Does that sound tasty?"

"My goodness! It sounds excellent!"

But the old man, who'd been listening without saying a thing, spoke up:

"Which chicken's neck will you twist?"

"There's no choice; they're all old, and the hens are brooding. We'll take the little red rooster..."

"Ah! no," said the old man, shaking his hand in a violent gesture of refusal. "Ah! no! You must never do that! You must never break up pairs. He has his hen, let him be."

As the man spoke, he'd maintained the frozen posture of blind men who speak without ever looking away, as they no longer see faces. Since the old woman and I remained silent, he went on:

"Listen well, Mister Jean, and understand me, because not even for you will I have that little rooster killed.

When you met me, despite my sixty years, I had good legs and a good eye. Never did I suspect that while living, I'd no longer see the light of our good Lord. The sickness took me one day when we went to receive friends from town. They'd arrived unannounced, for lunch, and we decided to fry up a little white hen we'd bought to brighten up the henhouse. I went to search for her myself; but when I carried her off, *her* rooster — it was like the creature understood — jumped on my legs, flew up to my hands, screamed, clawed, beat its wings. It seemed funny at first, I admit; but after five minutes, I no longer thought so. That evening, returning to the house, I realized that something like flies were dancing in my eyes. I thought it was tiredness. But at night, my head hurt, and in the morning, when it was time to go to the fields, it was like there was a fog before me. This went on for almost a week. Since I thought it was the sun doing me harm, I stayed home. When the heat went away, I went out to the pen for a chat with the creatures. They know me well, you know. In the barnyard, the chickens came to peck my hand. But the little white rooster ran away from me. As soon as I arrived, he flapped his wings and went to hide near the incubators. I remember that afterward I said to my wife:

"Look at the little rooster. It looks like he's afraid, like someone made his life miserable."

Today I remember that; but at the time I didn't pay it too much attention. Especially as my eyes wouldn't heal. This went on for two months, then I decided to consult a doctor in town. Right away he told me it was very serious. I was afraid, of course. Put yourself in my place...

"Do you think I'll lose my sight?"

He didn't say yes, he didn't say no, but he ordered me to rest on my back without moving, even to eat, for two or three months.

"At least, can you tell me if I'll heal?"

"Perhaps..."

Once I was back home, I wept my share. I suspect-
ed he didn't want to tell me everything, and that I was
going to go blind. I started to walk through the house
and the garden, looking at everything with wide eyes in
which flies were still dancing, as if I could somehow
shut away inside them everything I would soon no longer see: the furniture, our good bed, the cuckoo clock that
went tick-tock in its case, the old dog sleeping by the
turning spit, the trees in the garden and the flowers in
rows; the well where fresh water rose up in the summer,
the happy henhouse where creatures tapped their beaks
at gray stones, and the little white rooster which hid
when it saw me approach, the little rooster which was so
sad and had such drab feathers, such a pale crest...

... The next day, I began treatment. First I lay
down, then the blinds were closed, and finally, so I could
guide myself in the room, a small night lamp was placed
over the fireplace. That was the only source of light allowed to me. Ah! those days! I reflected so much, and
was so sad! I sank deep into my own head, in the attempt
to understand why the sickness had come...

One morning, the neighbors brought me a country
healer. He threw endless questions at me, and made an
awful lot of signs over my head, before asking suddenly:

"Have you ever hurt animals?"

All at once, the little rooster came to my mind. I
hadn't done anything to him, to be sure, but I'd taken his
hen. He'd defended her well, and wasted away ever
since!...

From that moment on, the rooster became an obsession. Every morning, I asked for news of the creature,
and the response was always a shrug:

"But he's alright! What makes you worry about him
so much?"

39

I never dared say, sir, what the matter really was. But it's certain that the little rooster no longer crowed, and that my sickness only kept getting worse. I saw the flame of the night lamp less clearly than in the first days.

One evening, my wife was lying beside me, and I was nodding off. After a moment, I woke up and saw nothing. Not a night lamp, not a glow. The noise I made then woke up my wife too:

"What do you want?" she asked. "Do you need anything?"

"No."

"Then go back to sleep, love."

"I'm not tired. What time is it?"

"I don't know."

You know how people get mean when they're ill. I said to her a little harshly:

"See what great care you take of me! You didn't even prepare the night lamp!..."

"What do you mean?"

"Look, it's gone out!"

She went quiet a moment, then said with a funny voice: "It's true... I'm sorry... Do you want me to get up?"

I felt bad for having pushed her around, and said: "No, there's no use. I don't need it, go to sleep..."

I stayed awake, listening to the clock tick. How long it lasts, a night without sleep! And that weak light from the night lamp I was used to was missing.

Little by little, a thought occurred to me: How could my wife, usually so careful, have forgotten the lamp?... And she'd answered me with such a strange voice. Perhaps she'd been half-asleep?... But no, she'd spoken with me before that... So?...

Was the night lamp lit and I couldn't see it?...

But it was… that was it… I was blind…

I called: "Hey, woman!"

Before the words were out of my mouth, she said to me in a very clear voice, like someone who wasn't asleep:

"What is it, love?"

"Are you sure the night lamp's gone out?"

She hesitated:

"Yes… but yes…"

"It's not true! I'm blind!"

"My poor man… my poor man…"

"Get up," I shouted… "Open the blinds… so I can check."

"But there's no use. It's not day yet…"

"Yes! yes! Get up! Open them!"

I heard the window creak and the shutters open.

"You see," she whispered, "it's night."

Ah! The good Lord! I breathed again. She had told me the truth! I had believed, so long had the hours seemed to me, that it was day, that the night lamp was burning but that I couldn't see it… But it was still night, good night!…

Then, Mister, in the silence, in my night, the little rooster, which had been mute for days, crowed! He crowed, in a triumphant voice that must have swelled up his throat and raised him up on his two little feet.

He crowed, and I realized that the day that I'd never see again had arrived, that the night lamp in the room had been lit, and that my wife had lied to me piously for hours, to delay the moment when I would learn everything!…

The rooster crowed with joy, perhaps because he knew I was blind, and I heard my poor old woman weeping…"

The Clock

Almost hidden in the depths of an uncultivated garden, its blinds still shuttered, its crumbling walls hot from the sun and washed by rains, its roof made of bricks with no smoke rising from the chimneys, the little country house that locals called the "House of Crime" was quite a strange place.

I'd always wanted to visit but never found a way, until one day I saw a sign hanging on the door with the words: "To let."

At first I thought it was a joke. But who knows what curiosity pushed me on, I rang the bell. It made a crackling sound like hail… Finally it seemed to me that there was a noise coming from the back of the house. I listened… There was the shuffling of dragging feet, the jingling of keys… the grinding of locks… and then the door, squealing on its hinges, opened.

An old man came toward me. He looked serious, ceremonious and dignified. His face showed no emotion, and his approach was slow: just the sort of strange inhabitant this house would have.

He undid the locks, opened the door and standing aside to let me pass, said in a flat voice:

"Is it about the rent, sir?"

On the off chance, I replied: "Yes".

Astonishment flashed in his eyes. He put his hand on the locks, and after having carefully closed the door again, muttered:

"Very good. Please follow me…"

The house itself had nothing particularly interesting to offer. Everything was so old, sad and run down there.

On the walls, the paper was torn off and hanging in places, showing the yellow plaster.

The frames of the frosted windows looked like they'd come from old prints, and the furniture, which seemed antique, was covered in a thick layer of dust. The trees of the garden filtered the light so well that the rooms only brightened slightly, with a faint glow, when we pushed open the shutters.

The master of the house led me through the apartment, closing every door after him silently and with care. In a few brief words, he informed me:

"Here's the bedroom to sleep. There's a bathroom. There, another bedroom. The linen closet is connected to the guest room. On the upper floor are the service quarters and attic."

Once the tour was over, I said mechanically — to say something:

"Is that all?"

He stopped, stared at me a long time as if my question had something unusual about it, then having chosen a key from his bunch, plunged it into a lock. He jiggled it until it opened, then answered me in a strange voice:

"No. There's still this room."

I went in. It was very dark there, and very damp. I made out a window fitted with thick bars, two stools and a square table pushed against a wall. He opened the blinds halfway, and in the weak light that came in, I could see, hanging from a hook on the ceiling, a rope with a knot in it. In a corner, there was a rustic clock so covered in dust it no longer had any color, but in spite of looking as if it hadn't been touched for many years, just like all the other objects in that house, it beat time with a mournful and regular tick-tock.

Immediately this simple clock caught my eye and imagination with such extraordinary force that the stranger's words quietly echoing hardly startled me.

"This is the room of the crime."

I turned to him. He was motionless; not a muscle of his face had moved. He added — and I thought I made out a sort of irony in his voice:

"For this is the House of Crime!…"

I looked at him, amazed, listening to the tick-tock of the clock behind him. He seemed to notice my surprise, or paleness, and after gesturing toward one of the stools, he sat on the other and continued:

"I'm telling you this, sir, for I didn't believe for a minute that you came here to rent… Don't protest!… You've come here to see this… And you've seen it… You've come here to know… Well! Now you'll know…

It always seems ridiculous when a man of my age — I'm almost eighty — speaks of love. Yet it's a love story that I'm going to tell you. It dates back more than half a century. Here it goes: I got married very young — I wasn't yet twenty-three — to a woman I loved madly, and who loved me the same way — or at least so I thought. In order to avoid disturbances, and to enjoy my happiness in peace, I'd bought this little house, and we came to live here. To be quite honest, I'll tell you that in that sort of exile there was maybe something more than just the desire to find a place for our honeymoon. There was also a vague need to remove my woman from the temptations of this world, for I could get fiercely jealous. We lived there for a few months, before one day I was called to the side of a sick parent.

What follows is the eternal story of adultery. I came back earlier than expected… than she expected. I opened the door unsuspecting, heard a confused murmur of voices, and then as if by magic, all the lights went out... I rushed toward the stairs... there was a shape fleeing... I threw myself after it, and there, behind the door of that room, I seized the fugitive by the collar. While I held him up with a fist against the wall, I fumbled in my pocket, struck a match and saw before me a half-dressed man with bare feet, struggling under my grip.

At first I thought I was dealing with a thief, but the disorder of his appearance created a terrible suspicion in me... I called out:

"Louise! Louise!"

Nothing... Dragging the man by the throat, I went to the end of the hallway, and at the bottom of the stairway, I glimpsed my wife. She was disheveled, wearing just a shirt, and when she saw me, she began to scream: "Mercy! Mercy!..."

... As I'm an oversensitive and jealous person, I'd thought in calmer hours of what my attitude would be if I surprised my wife in a lover's arms. I'd always told myself: "It would be too much for me... I'd kill them with kicks, with punches!..."

Well... it didn't happen that way at all!... Instead of the impulsive and wild gesture I expected to make, a frightening calm prevented me from giving way to instinct. A cold, rational hatred froze my fury, and my mind was lucid enough to understand that killing them at that moment would be a poor revenge. In their fear, they wouldn't feel my blows. And so, resolved on crime — but learned, refined crime — I grabbed them both like old rags and pushed them into this room. Once I saw them on the ground, panting, I leaned over them, and without a shout, without a gesture, said:

"You wanted to have a private chat? Have at it

then! I'll leave you here. But take good advantage of your moment of love! It's midnight. At four o'clock by this clock, I'll kill you like dogs!..."

Then I went out, closing the door with a double lock. I went up to my study, and there, all alone, suffered an explosion of pain, sobbing for a long time, head in my hands.

Suddenly, the little clock on the mantelpiece struck... One... two... three... I looked at the dial. But no! A quarter to four had just struck... I passed my hand before my eyes as if waking from a dream, and to reaffirm my resolve, said:

"Come on! You must punish them now!..."

In the drawer of my desk, I grabbed my revolver and slipped in six cartridges. Then I took a candelabra and went down...

I must have been a frightful sight, but I didn't tremble. On the stairs I listened closely... Such silence hung over the whole house that I wondered for a second: "Could they have fled?..."

When I went into the hallway, I could still hear nothing, except the deep tick-tock of the clock that on the lower floor was marking time for the wretched. I set my candelabra on the ground and looked at my watch: four o'clock!... With a decisive gesture, I seized the key... when a peal of laughter... a peal of terrible, superhuman laughter came to my ears... I stood there for a second strangled with fear... Silence... I believed I'd been the victim of some hallucination and violently opened the door.

Then, sir, I saw a frightening thing:

A rope tied around his neck, the man was swinging in the void, and in a corner crouched like a beast, eyes haggard and biting her nails, my wife stared at me. All of a sudden, she began to laugh, that terrible laugh that had frozen me just before. She laughed deeply, then went silent. Her face suddenly took on an expression of indescribable anguish. She turned toward a corner of the room, and looked at something I couldn't see, saying some incoherent words, among which one repeated, always the same, the one she kept coming back to:

"The clock!... The clock!..."

I had come to perform justice, but now I stood there frightened, between the hanged man and that mad lady, moaning over and over: "The clock... The clock!..." This ending was inexplicable. Was I to believe the man had been so cowardly as to commit suicide, not daring face my vengeance, leaving his only accomplice in front of me?...

... The dirty glow of the emerging dawn slipped gently into the room.

Suddenly, my wife let out a cry, stretching out her arms:

"There! There!..."

My eyes mechanically followed her gesture, but before me I saw nothing except the clock.

At first, I didn't understand. Then, something very simple about its appearance struck me: the clock was ticking. Within the high case, the tick-tock echoed like a heart in a chest. The large white face of the clock stood out against the darkness, and you could read the numbers on it...

But the face of the clock did not have hands!...

Suddenly the truth dawned on me, and the terrible agony of the two became clear. I followed them, I lived with them in thought, and now I could explain how things had gone. I'd told them: "At four o'clock by this clock, I'll kill you." Once the door was shut, they'd tried

47

to flee, but they realized it was impossible, that all their efforts would be in vain. Their brains went empty with fear, as they knew that every tick-tock was a note that drew a drop of their blood. Then, losing their heads, with that remnant of instinct that makes the condemn cling for existence to the foot of the scaffold, they'd wanted to take advantage of what time remained to them to live. They'd rushed to see the clock... but the clock without hands, the clock that knew the time and pounded relentlessly back and forth, no longer wanted to reveal its secret. She kept it in her belly, and hid it well!... They watched it breathe, counted its beats, heard its mournful song, but did not understand.

And so the seconds became for them hours, nights, centuries! Every sound was perhaps the last... Every time the pendulum tripped, they felt the anguish of the massacre. With every swing, they thought they would see this door open... They died a hundred times that way, a thousand times, torn to shreds, to scraps!... Ah! I hadn't planned this ordeal for them, this torment as great as Fate that choked off slowly, with a heavy hand, ruthlessly, their heart, their skin, their reason.

No man knows how to punish like this, sir, and at that moment I blessed heaven.

Of course I was arrested and tried. At court I felt no need to explain events... I had so little left in life... Yet my hour must not yet have come, for although accused — and convicted — of murder, I benefited from the mitigating circumstances, and was condemned to only five years in prison!

Afterward, I came back here. Everything remains as it was before. No one lives near me anymore except that clock, which I wind up religiously. Sometimes I sit for hours contemplating its empty face... I talk to it... The truth is, I believe that objects have a soul, since at times this clock face seems to look at me — but now it's over. The clock can rest; my wife died two years ago in a madhouse.

Other people will live within these walls... They will have their sadnesses here... their joys... None will enjoy the bitter pleasures of revenge more than I have..."

He went on speaking for a long time... It was getting dark... Shadows ranged over the dusty gray walls.

There was the clock with its empty face, the clock that had seen such frightening things, the clock crying in its wooden case...

The Bad Guide

How long had passed, days, weeks or months, since he'd been rotting at the bottom of this low pit?... The man couldn't say.

No ray entered his cell, completely in shadow. With the help of his knees and hands, he'd raised up on his bed mounted on the wall and touched the ceiling of the prison. But his fingers did not find in those smooth walls, or in the wet paving stones, or the door with rusty irons, the slightest hole or gap.

At first, he'd thought that his eyes would grow used to the cruel night to eventually distinguish objects there, that his reason would come to the aid of his aggravated senses so he'd be able to perceive, amidst the darkness, a bit of the intangible soul of day that never entirely disappears for the living.

But his wide-open eyes had cried in vain at night, his eyelids had bled with the useless effort. Everything was black, everything remained dark.

He didn't hear, in this tomb that dragged on his slow agony, the steps of the jailer who from time to time brought him his meager fare. For a second, the door of his cell would open slightly. His blinking eyes would see the red mark of a lantern, and the paler mark of a leaning face or hand held out, as the shadow of the hallways mingled with the impenetrable shadow of his cell. Then, the door would close again. The sound of footsteps in the corridors would go away, growing softer, and once again great silence would thicken his night.

Sometimes he could also hear the wind howl, and the monotonous lapping of water, which beat against the walls of the dungeon in the moats. Wild dreams of sky, freedom and light had at first haunted his restless sleep. Then, the light disappeared even from his dreams. There only remained the sole obsession of escaping from this sepulcher. Plans became mixed up in his confused head, with everything leading to the same goal: Escape!

One day — or one night, he could not have said — as he was thinking, seated on his bunk, the sound of the jailer's steps pulled him from his torpor. Although he had long ceased to feel the slightest emotion at the approach of this living person, his stomach was crying out in hunger, and his parched lips needed to quench their thirst. So he stood up and began to walk, groping his way forward.

A rush of fresh air brought him the sharp smell of damp stone. By the light of the lantern, he saw his pitcher and bowl set down. The half-opened door closed again. He stretched out his hand toward the stone jug, but at the moment he grabbed it, he stopped: a strange cry had pierced the silence. He waited, thinking he'd misheard. He took a step: the same cry came up from the ground. He kneeled down, gently smacking his lips, as if calling a dog. Nothing answered. Crawling on all fours, he felt the paving stones around him. Having found the pitcher, he took it and began to drink with big gulps, then set it down in a corner.

Suddenly the touch of something clammy and cold startled him. Under his hand, something seemed to breathe, and the cry that had surprised him a moment before rose up, flute-like, strange. He remained without moving, his fist clenched on the sticky mass that seemed to throb, pulsing quick and rhythmic between his fingers.

Once again, the cry echoed in his ears. The thing curled up under his grip, trying to escape. Then, in the midst of his disgust and anguish, it began to glow. Despite himself, he said, almost out loud:

"It's a beast!…"

The sound of his own voice frightened him.

He repeated:

"It's a beast… a beast…"

And suddenly he shivered in every limb, sweat beading on his forehead. There was no doubt: the strange cry, the sticky body… that cry, that body, belonged to a toad. A toad!… He imagined seeing the horrible beast, the unclean thing with its striped back, white belly and big golden eyes.

His fingers loosened their grip. The toad fell with a soft thud.

Then, his fearful instinct and spitefulness woke at once, and he wanted to crush it with a stamp of his heel. His foot struck the flabby beast, and he thought he'd killed it.

But the toad, mutilated without being dead, began to cry out again. The man chased it, striking the ground with his open palms.

Mixed with his deep disgust was the dark remorse of the executioner. He wanted to kill the beast, not simply so as not to risk brushing against it again, but also to muffle its complaints. The effort was useless. The cry repeated… here… there… and each time his fingers thought they'd grasped the beast, they met with nothing but the icy paving stone or the rough wall.

Exhausted, knees swollen and palms bloody, he lay down on his bunk and fell asleep.

When he woke up, he thought:

"The beast must be dead."

He listened. For a moment, he heard nothing but the distant moaning of the wind. Relieved, he breathed more deeply. He got up, and still groping, made his way to the door. For a long time, with the help of an old piece of iron hidden in a corner, he tried to wear down the hinges. He resumed his patient work, scraping away without noise.

Suddenly, the cry of the toad rose up:

"Ah! vile beast," snarled the prisoner, "I'll shut you up!" He began his hunt again, in vain. As soon as he thought he had the beast, it slipped through his fingers.

This lasted for days and days. If he wasn't working to tear down the door, he was crawling in search of the invisible toad. The call of the wounded creature sounded at regular intervals. And at such moments, the captive, exasperated and sweating with fear, felt his reason disturbed. Ah! What a pleasure it would be to crush that monster, to see it burst under his boot!...

Almost delirious, he insulted and provoked it:

"Come here then! Come here!... Show yourself!... Dare to show yourself!..."

... Now it happened that by filing down the hinges of the door, they at last gave way. By beating and pivoting heavily, the prisoner was able to open it.

A door!... What was that next to the awful barriers he'd no doubt have to cross before seeing the day again!... Yet an infinite joy restored his courage. He thought:

"Since God has allowed me to destroy the first obstacle with my hands, perhaps he also wants the others to collapse before me."

The corridor that receded between the thick walls was nearly as dark as his dungeon. But his eyes made out a light, coming from somewhere he didn't know, which softened the night. His heart beat to burst his chest, and he listened. Not a sound. He said:

"The jailer is sleeping… The tired guards, no doubt, are sleeping too… Let's go!"

He took a step:

"Which way?… Right?… or left?… Minutes are worth centuries… one second is a fortune… I can't lose a single one… which side are the exits on? Which side should I make my way toward, before I flee through open country?"

He understood that he was in danger of getting lost, that likely he wouldn't find an exit, that he might throw himself in the arms of his executioners. An impotent rage brought tears to his eyes. He roared:

"Oh! all my useless reason for a flash of instinct!" He clenched his fingers in his hair, his nails dug into his skin.

And here, at the same moment, the mournful cry of the toad echoed. In the faint light that had just blessed his eyes, he saw its slimy body shining. Tenderness filled him, and he looked at the hated animal as a savior. He stood on tiptoe so as not to obstruct its path, guessing the creature would move by instinct toward the light, and that by following the filthy trace of its path over the paving stones, he'd find his way toward radiant day.

Formerly crippled, the toad advanced with awkward hops. He didn't take his eyes off it, watching its trail. He crawled behind it through the hallways, climbing and descending stairs, muttering in the tone of prayer:

"Go… go… Lead me…"

Suddenly a cool breeze caressed his face, and before him he could see a patch of sky cut away where the stars were just ceasing to shine. In the distance, a ray of snowy light fringed with clouds was appearing. His two hands clasped, he wept.

Then, shaking with emotion, he stretched out a leg, and his foot slipped. He put out the other, and it slipped as well. The ground seemed to give way beneath him and he sank down to his ankles. He tried to free his trapped feet but only sank more quickly. He was bogged down now up to the knees. He stretched out his hands, but his hands, which seemed to be resting on solid earth, were swallowed by thick mud… He sank and sank… He wanted to call out, but his voice died in his throat. The mud was rising. It came up to his hips… sucked him in up to his stomach, then up to his armpits, grazed his chin, came to brush his lips…

With a final effort, as he opened his mouth wide to scream, he heard the cry that had obsessed his vigils, and felt a soft body press against his pale face. Before him, belly swollen, legs outstretched, he saw the fat toad skip away over the foul mud and water.

The man moaned:

"Ah! You're taking revenge!…"

Then he closed his eyes, gasped "Mea culpa!" and disappeared.

… From the pond, which had suddenly woken up, joyous croaks could be heard… Night was dying at the edge of the changing sky. The ripples in the marsh water widened in the shadows… then the water was still once more.

A night bird, fleeing swiftly before day came, skimmed the dark surface of the pond in its flight.

Then, through the gray rain, dawn at last slowly hoisted itself up on the horizon.

Fascination

An hour ago I was a prisoner. And what a prisoner! It wasn't my freedom or honor that was at stake: it was my head.

I'd known the terrified sleep full of nightmares of the guillotine. With terror I'd passed sweating hands over my cold neck, guessing the narrow path the blade would trace there. I'd shuddered at the hostile murmurs of the crowd. In my ears, I'd heard the shout: "To death!"

With a single word, all that has vanished. I'm free. Once again I'm here in the noisy streets, and can see the light of the shops. In a while I'll dine, completely at my ease. Sitting by the fire, I'll smoke my pipe, and tonight I'll go to sleep calmly, lying down in the warm bed waiting for me.

Yet I never felt so criminal as at the moment the judges came to absolve me. I wonder by what aberration they've failed to see the person I really am. Since I'm prohibited from making a denial, to recover my spirits, I'll write down the truth concealed for three months with such cynicism that at times even I was taken in by my lies.

For in truth, I am a murderer: I killed a woman.

Why?... I've never known exactly.

Not out of jealousy, in any case: I didn't love her. Nor to steal: I'm rich, and the few francs that I found on her didn't tempt me. Not out of anger, either...

We were in this room. She was standing before that

mirror; I was seated, just as I am now, reading. She said:

"Let's go down... We'll take a walk in the park."

Without looking up, I answered:

"No, I'm tired. Let's stay."

She insisted. I was stubborn in my refusal. She insisted again, and her voice annoyed me. She spoke in an angry tone, cutting her sentences with small unpleasant laughs, shrugging her shoulders. Several times I tried to interrupt:

"Shut up, will you?... Shut up, I beg you..."

She continued. I got up and began to walk through the room, and while walking I saw a small revolver on the mantelpiece that I was in the habit of carrying in the evening. Mechanically, I picked it up. From the second I had it in my hands, something strange happened. The voice of my mistress, which had only irritated me at first, now exasperated me to a degree I cannot express. It wasn't the words she uttered, but her voice, her voice alone. If she'd said the words out of sequence or in the most beautiful verse, I would've felt the same tension. A necessity for peace, for absolute calm, came over me. How, why was a connection established in my head between the revolver I was holding, and the silence that remained out of reach?... This connection, this relationship, still needs to be clarified. I saw myself pointing the gun and pulling the trigger, and saw the woman falling without a cry.

Occasionally, these kind of dizzy hallucinations can pass through the mind, without thought stopping there. But this time, it seemed that in passing, the vision had suddenly caught on my reason, like a nail catches on silk, and that it got further tangled the more violently I tried to tear it out. I put the revolver on the table. I couldn't take my eyes off it. I wanted to look away, but

57

my gaze kept returning.

There it was, before me, a little inanimate thing, with its ivory grip, cylinder and shiny barrel. Two, three times I moved forward, then withdrew my hand. It was stronger than me. A need came to me to grasp it, to touch it.

Occasionally, in situations of danger, one has inexplicable temptations. I remember that one day, at the park in Buttes-Chaumont, I had to cling to the parapet, in that place called the Bridge of Suicides, so as not to throw myself into the abyss. Other times, finding myself alone on the train, I felt the morbid desire to pull the alarm. That handful of nickel called out to me, attracted me. No matter how much I told myself that the act I would commit was absurd, that I would be given a severe punishment, if a sudden stop or passing train had not violently redirected my thought, I'm convinced I would have succumbed to the temptation.

Well! At that moment, I felt the same dizziness. My eyes and hands no longer obeyed my will. I looked at myself as if another were acting, whose gestures I had to follow, without understanding where they'd lead.

Was she speaking?... Had she shut up?... I don't know. The only perception and memory I clearly retain is that with the gun in my hand, I walked toward her, that my hand rose and that when it was at the height of her chest, I fired. This made a noise like the crack of a whip, and then I saw a red mark, very small, above her right eye. The woman fell, limp, like a petticoat that when unhooked falls to the ground.

Suddenly, reason came back to me. A wild terror seized me. I threw down the revolver and ran like a madman through the room, without even thinking of leaning over my victim. I don't know what instinct of low cowardice compelled me, but I opened the door and raced down the stairs, shouting:

"Help!… She killed herself!…"

At first, everyone believed it was a suicide. Then the experts found that too improbable, and I was arrested. The investigation lasted a long time. With a single sentence, I could have explained everything. I only had to say:

"Here's what happened."

But I persisted in denial, obstinate. And since in the end, a motive must always be attributed to a criminal act and none could be found against me, I was acquitted.

I consider all this in cold blood now, and ask myself if I was not wrong to lie. If I'd told those jurors what I'm writing here, would they have believed me? Would they have absolved me? I think of them so often I could be mistaken for one of them…

… My God, it is so good to be free, to come and go as I please!

From my window, I see the street, the houses, the trees… It's here that the tragedy happened. They didn't want to take me back to this room, and I had to find my way myself. I don't believe in ghosts. But I knew that to record these notes, it would be better for me to be here. It seems memories awaken more easily in the places where they're formed.

… Really, this confession has made me recover completely. My soul is clear now, clean, as if it's been washed.

I'll try to forget this bad dream. I'll live in the country, far from Paris. My name will be forgotten. I'll be another man, with a new life, wearing peasant clothes… I'll no longer recognize myself.

There's one thing above all that I don't want to

keep: this revolver, given back to me just now by the administrative office of the court. It reminds me too painfully of past hours. If I need a gun, I'll buy another.

There it rests before me as I write, and the sight of it pains me. Yet it's such a small thing!... and so lovely... it looks like a jewel, a pretty trinket... when you look at it that way, it doesn't seem dangerous...

... Let me come and take it in my hand. It's so light and smooth. It's also very cold... it scares me a little... it's mysterious, this sleeping gun... with a knife, you see the threat, the sharp point and cutting blade... here, nothing. You have to know... I don't want to keep it... I'll sell it, tomorrow... Oh! Sell it?... I'll give it away... Not even that! No! I'll throw it...

In any case, I don't want to see it for some time. I look at it too much... that's only natural, isn't it?... there it is, like a silent witness... it's decided, I won't keep it another hour...

... I'm still writing, with this gun before me...

People who commit suicide must record their last wishes like this. What feelings could they experience?... I imagine that they are strong, as they do it. They dare not look... at first. Then, their resolution made, who knows if, on the contrary, they can't their eyes off the pistol?... if they're not irresistibly attracted, fascinated?...

Really, do you need so much courage to kill yourself? The hardest thing must be the simple gesture of stretching out your hand and picking up the weapon, feeling how cold it is...

... So! I hold it in my left hand... I press the barrel against my temple... it's not an entirely disagreeable feeling... a very slight shudder... then the steel heats in contact with my flesh...

No, it's not that which must be the most terrifying part... it must be the second you fire... the last order given by a person to the thing...

... But who knows?... perhaps that too is nothing?... dizziness overtakes you, and you feel irresistibly attracted.

This doesn't feel bad...

... It's nothing...

... I feel nothing...

... the unknown is calling...

... you just press... clamp...

... and pull the trigger...

Mitigating Circumstances

It was from the newspaper that Françoise learned of the arrest of her boy.

The thing seemed so monstrous to her at first that she didn't even want to believe it.

Her boy, her little boy, so polite, so shy, who'd come a month earlier to spend Easter holidays with her; her boy, a thief and a killer?... She could see him now! In his infantryman's uniform, with his good figure... she could still feel the brush of his goodbye kiss on her wrinkled cheeks, and with her gentle and peaceful memories so vivid, she could only shrug and repeat to herself:

"There must have been an error, it's not him."

Yet there it was, written clearly in big letters: "A criminal soldier." It had happened in his small garrison, and it spelled out his full name.

She froze in dismay, lifted her glasses onto her forehead and clasped her hands together. Trembling, she spoke to herself in the warm silence of the kitchen, looking at without seeing the old dog dozing by the open door and the clock in its case, marking the time with a grave, drawling tick-tock...

Someone came in. Startled, she asked:

"Who's there?"

Recognizing a neighbor, and not wanting her to guess the problem, she added:

"I was sleeping... It's so hot..."

Usually a bit silent and reserved, she talked on and on, asking questions and answering out of the fear she'd be questioned, wondering as she produced her broken sentences:

"Does she know?…"

At last she went quiet, not finding any more words. With a strange look, her neighbor asked her:

"Has it been long since you've had news of your son?"

"No… This morning."

Françoise didn't say how! All at once, a great need came to her to be comforted, reassured, to hear another voice than her own protest in outrage: "It's a mistake! It's not him, how could you imagine!…"

She showed her neighbor the newspaper, and made an effort to sound amused:

"Have you read it?… that's funny, isn't it?"

Throat dry, tears in her eyes, she added:

"It's silly, anyway… when I first saw it, I had a shock!… of course I did!…"

The neighbor stayed silent. She repeated:

"It's funny, right?… it's funny…"

"Yes, it is funny that there are two men with exactly the same name in the same regiment."

With a sigh, the old woman exclaimed:

"I told myself the same thing!… can you imagine… there are two… he's not mine!…"

"But you know, there's gossip. I ask you… it'd be desirable… because the assumption is that it was him… they already say he was the one who gave the blow to the cooper… Yes, 300 francs were stolen, when he was on leave."

The mother, completely pale, stood up and clenched her fists:

"They can talk!… it's not him, no, it's not him… you have no shame!… what did we do to you, that

63

makes you go after us?... poor little one!... you'll see!..."

And without closing the door behind her, without even changing into boots, she ran to the station.

She arrived in the city at the seven pm. During the trip, her terror only increased. Now she no longer said "It's impossible!" but "What if it were true...!" The road seemed endless, and the countryside, fields, telegraph poles and face of her boy all seemed to rise and fall before her in a dizzying sway. When the train stopped, she began to tremble, finding that the moment when she'd at last know was near, and too quickly arrived.

She murmured her *Pater* and *Ave*, adding supplications to the prayers that mechanically came to her lips:

"Oh! Holy Virgin, you didn't want this, isn't that right?... The beautiful prayers that I'll send you later!..."

Behind the gate, the courtyard of the barracks stretched out, all white, with square buildings. The soldiers were seated on the doorstep, chatting in the calm night. Her little one had known these men. With great humility, she asked:

"Excuse me, Mister Sergeant, I'd like to ask you for a quick word. Here it is..."

She hesitated, not daring to state her real fear right away.

"Here it is... this report against my son... Michon, Jules, in 3rd company... I'd like to know if... I could see him..."

She tried to smile:

"I'm his mother... his mama... no? Well!... Where is he then?... He's not ill, is he?... Then?... Do I know?... No, no... I don't know... Has he been punished?... In a police room?... No?... In... in prison...

you say?... He'll appear in front of a military tribunal?..."

She hid her face in her hands:

"Good Lady, it was true then! Good Lady!..."

She walked away, almost staggering. At the military prison, she was told her little one was in solitary, and that word solitary increased her terror even more. She saw him alone, forever separated from the world, sick. She was told to go see her lawyer, and though she didn't dare hear what he had to say, she went. He said she already knew the whole truth. Doubt was no longer possible. Her little one had killed to steal, and the money — almost six hundred francs — had been found in his mattress... He'd finally confessed.

Once she'd cried and begged to be allowed to see him, in vain, she returned to her village. Everyone knew. Fearing the words and looks, she went back home at night. Like a poor animal that fears beatings and remains in hiding, she didn't dare go out, keeping her blinds closed and trembling as each morning she picked up the newspaper slid under her door.

So she went on reading all the details of the crime and all the accusations against her child. People appeared before the judge, and all of them suggested it was the Michon boy who had stolen from the cooper... but it wasn't true! She'd swear it... And then she began to doubt even that.

After a month, she went back to the lawyer. Now she no longer asked to see her son, not that she'd stopped loving him, great God!... She was ashamed...

"What are they going to do to him, good sir? You won't let them take him from me..."

"My poor woman, I'm afraid... if only I could find a mitigating circumstance..."

"What is that you said? A circumstance... what does that mean?..."

"It means something that would diminish his guilt in the eyes of the judges. Take a man who steals, for example; if you could prove that poverty pushed him to do it, that while it is true he stole it was to give bread to his children, well! That is a mitigating circumstance. Same for him! This is not even his first attempt. That other theft — he denies it — but... well, I'll do all that is humanly possible to try." Françoise returned more tired and pained than ever, her mind tortured by those new words: "Mitigating circumstances." How she wanted to find it, that excuse to which a bit of pardon might cling!... But nothing. Only the crime was evident, monstrously so, nothing could lessen the horror...

The day of judgment arrived. She set off again, to complete her cavalry. On the train she prayed, invoking all of the saints, and in her empty head those words, repeated so often, echoed: "Mitigating circumstances... mitigating circumstances..."

She waited in a sad room, with witnesses who spoke in low voices in front of her. When her turn came, she walked unsteadily, blinking under the overly bright light, and immediately her gaze fell on the boy who, head down, holding a handkerchief with big blue squares in his fingers, was crying in short sobs... Then she braced herself before the judges.

She'd wanted to appear. Now she wondered why... She knew nothing, she was just an old lady, she had nothing to say!... Who was she anyway?... No one. The mother of her little one, that's all. She'd given birth to him, yes... cradled him, yes... brought him up, yes... He was hers then... But no, today he was no longer hers.

She replied to all questions with signs or unintelligible words. A great silence hung over the room. An infinite pity descended on this peasant in mourning, slumped over in grief.

"Is he your only child?" asked the president.

"Yes, sir."

"When he was at home, did you have reason to complain of him?"

"Oh no! Sir…"

"Were you aware of him keeping bad company?"

"Never. Neither his father, whom all the world loved and respected, nor I, would allow… one could say we were held in high esteem, you know!…"

"We know, we know…"

Then, turning to the accused:

"You knew it too, and that's why you felt safe. Hiding behind your parents' honor, you took advantage of the stay at your mother's house to steal… How could one suspect the son of such good people?… Some might say: 'I'm only half responsible. The bad examples before me were what did me in.' You don't even have that excuse."

When she heard this, the old woman made a strong effort to control herself. In her tiny eyes, where tears quivered on the eyelashes, a strange gleam passed. Head bowed, without a gesture, with a voice that hardly trembled anymore, she spoke.

"Excuse me, sir. I must tell you the truth. My little one is guilty, very guilty, it's true… But he's not the only one… Just now, I told you that I'd never done anything I could be reproached for… I lied. The three hundred francs at the cooper's, it was me who stole them… me… When my little one came home on leave, I confessed to him… So my child got scared… he told himself his mother had lost her honor and reputation… and to return the money, so no one made a complaint, he went back... Well, he panicked... he was surprised... and the misfortune occurred."

She went silent a moment, feeling suffocated. Then, in a lower tone:

"I lied... I'm a bad woman. It's I who have been a bad example... You should arrest me... That is a mitigating circumstance for him, isn't it?... Excuse me, sir..."

More curved than before, her shoulders more humble and her head lower, she looked small, so small...

... The son was only condemned to hard labor for life. She died soon after, cast out by the whole village. A quick mass was said for her, then her body was buried in the bare earth at the far end of the cemetery, in a corner where the shade of the church and bell tower did not reach, even on the most beautiful days.

This story was told to me next to her grave, adorned only by a black wood cross with a crown of rust-colored pearls, twisted and broken. It had been ruined by time, but nevertheless I could read these words engraved:

To Françoise Michon — Your son's judge.

The Well

Sitting on his doorstep, legs apart, both hands resting on the top of his cane, the old man kept his silence, that peasant silence which may be full of memories, or dull and thoughtless.

The day was ending. The distant cry of barn animals rose up into the softening sky. An old horse passed, returning all alone to its stable, dragging its harnesses behind it on the road.

The old man followed it with his eyes, shook his head and sighed:

"When I'm that age, you won't see me on these paths anymore!..."

"Is he so old as that?" I asked.

"Twenty years old at least. That would be eighty years old for a man."

"And why won't you live until then?"

"Why?... Look at me. I'm barely fifty... You thought I was older?... But yes! Fifty years old, and I can't work... I can barely stand on these legs."

"Did you suffer a serious illness?..."

"No. You know, I've never even been to the doctor. But!" — he struck his wrinkled forehead with his fist — "but it isn't easy... you don't make it to any golden wedding without certain memories. There are some hours that count more than years. Here, I'll tell you my story: you judge for yourself.

It must have been twenty-five years ago. Going to town I met the wife of a farmer from a neighboring village. Her husband was old — a good ten years older than me. The woman was my age. When you're young, you give little thought to the consequences... Anyway, even if I had thought about it, not a thing would have changed, seeing as when love speaks, it chases reason away...

One night I was with her, as her husband had gone in the morning to take the bullocks to the fair. Then I heard a noise in the house... I jumped to my feet... I slid on my shoes and jacket... I came down the stairs on tip-toe, crossed through the room below and the pigpen out front ... but I hadn't gone ten steps when two shots of a shotgun came from behind me.

By instinct, I threw myself face down. I wasn't hurt... not a scratch. But as I was getting up, I saw her husband leaning over me, waving his shotgun to knock me out. I started to run as fast as I could, and he launched after me, screaming:

"Scoundrel!... Crook!... Thief!... Stop!..."

In open country, I would have quickly escaped him, since my legs were better than his, and when running you have better lungs at twenty than forty. But there, in that garden I didn't know, he had the advantage. I stumbled against an iron fence and tripped over the melon beds, and every time I got up I could hear his voice even closer, crying out:

"Stop!... Stop!..."

At last I came to the hedge. I tore my face and hands, but I crossed it, racing down the hill with all the speed in my legs. But he'd taken a shortcut, and blocked my way just as I was entering an abandoned farm where I'd thought to dodge him. He rushed at me with kicks and punches, and I struck out too, like a madman. I took him by the throat; he stopped hitting and grabbed me around the waist. He squeezed, trying to crush the air out of me; I saw the eyes pop out of his head. My legs got tangled up in his. He tried to bite…

All of sudden, the ground gave way under our feet. He opened his arms… I let go of him… I heard his scream of terror and mine at the same time… I was falling… falling… then under my arm, under my armpit, I felt a terrible pain.

It seemed I'd been caught in mid-air… When I came to, at first I didn't even understand where I was, or how I was being held… Something was tearing the flesh of my shoulder and arm. My feet were dangling into an abyss… I opened my eyes and saw something below me, shining, something black and trembling, in which little lights danced. I tried to move my arms. But the movement I attempted to the left made me scream with pain. — I stretched out my right arm and with my open palm knocked against a cold wall, wet and sticky. My heels hit a wall too, and each kick made a deep sound, like a stone hitting an empty barrel.

Once my eyes began to get used to the darkness, I could see before me, so close that if I'd held out my hand I'd have brushed it, a black shape hanging from the wall, shuddering…

Little by little, in what had first been a confused mass, I made out arms… legs… and a head… a frightful head with the eyes rolled up, and the mouth twisted… the head of the man who just before, I'd been grappling with!…

Only then did I understand. During our struggle, we'd stood on planks that covered the mouth of a long abandoned well. Those planks, no doubt rotten, had given way under our weight, and in our fall, we'd been caught by two hooks, you know, the kind once put in wells to hang baskets so that bottles of water could cool, to avoid unwinding the rope all the way to the bottom. We were caught, skewered, closed in like sheep in a stall: me by the armpit, him — I could see him now — by the side, his stomach torn, his body hanging: on one side, legs and thighs — on the other, torso, head and arms...

Until then I hadn't heard any noise but the one I'd made myself, struggling. — The other, opposite me, began to gasp, and in the well, his rattle seemed to stretch out and echo in a frightening way... At the same time, I heard small splashes... toc... toc... toc... like water falling drop by drop into a beaker... The man was bleeding slowly into the water from his terrible wound... I don't know why though, but hearing his groan made me less afraid. You understand, I felt someone or something was with me...

This lasted a long time, a very long time, for the darkness began to fade. Morning came slowly... The darkness got lighter and lighter... The man's breaths became shorter. I could clearly see the smallest details on his awful head... his hands with crooked fingers... the drops of blood that made circles in the still water of the well. Then, his groaning began to get slower. The body jerked one or two more times, and it seemed that his head turned violently toward me. His eyes searched for mine, the mouth opened to shout once again: Scoundrel!... Crook!... Then nothing... not even the sound of drops... silence...

Faced with his death, fear, a terrible fear, took hold of me. I no longer felt my pain. Only one thought was in my head: I was alone there, lost. No one would think to look for me in that well. I'd die of suffering and hunger. Shout? Call for help? What good would that do! There was no road nearby... But I shouted anyway! I called for help... Nothing... No one answered.

By now day had completely arrived. The sun must have been high on the horizon. The patch of sky I could make out was blue, without a cloud... I shivered with anxiety and cold. I felt, or guessed, that the earth was hot, very hot, since we were in the first days of August.

I no longer dared to look at his still body. I no longer dared to risk a movement or gesture, so much did the slightest tremor cause me unbearable pain and suffering.

Then, in my ears, I heard a buzzing, which became increasingly clearer, and closer. It seemed blades of grass were brushing my face, and I opened my eyes. Ah! It wasn't a dream, it was a nightmare! I really had heard something, and what buzzed around me were flies, hundreds or thousands of them, flying around the motionless body next to mine!

I don't know how long that lasted. I only know that I was going crazy. While I still had my powers of reason, I realized that noon had come, that the sun was moving away... The body that the flies were dancing around seemed to lower imperceptibly... slipping down further... and further... I heard a sound of fabric being torn... The body descended more quickly and there was a scraping noise... like the sound of a brick dragged across uneven stones... then the violent sound of something heavy falling in the water... Drops splashed on me, and I opened my eyes.

The body had disappeared. In its place was a very red hook, on which a bit of cloth was swaying... After that I don't remember anything.

Afterward, I was told by a child that he'd been passing by and leaned over to throw some stones, when he saw me and called for help. If I calculate right, I'd been there nearly eighteen hours.

Now I wonder if he wouldn't have done better to let me die. My body healed, but I can say that not an hour goes by without that scene passing before my eyes. For twenty-five years I've had before me that man hanging from his side, for twenty-five years I've seen his face and ripped body, for twenty-five years I've felt the splash of the water drops in the well...

"And the woman?" I asked.

He said in a whisper.

"Mad."

He let out a long sigh:

"Ah! I am old, very old!"

... Night had fallen almost imperceptibly. Mist floated over the countryside. From the distance, there came the sound of a bell...

The man took off his hat, kneeled, made the sign of the cross and said to me in a low voice:

"This is the hour he fell..."

Everything was silent, but it seemed the echo of the bell could still be heard. At the end of the road, a couple of lovers walked slowly. — The old man kept praying, beating his chest...

The Miracle

It had come very slowly. First he'd felt before his eyes something like a veil, then shadows that occasionally darkened all objects. The first time, he'd passed his hands over his eyes and paid it no attention, telling himself: It's from working in the light too much. He rested a little. But imperceptibly, the veil thickened; the shadows lengthened and became larger. Without daring to admit it, he grew afraid.

One evening after dinner, everything in the room seemed completely dark to him, despite the big fire built from logs, and the lamp. He said to his wife:

"Raise the wick; we can't see a thing in here..."

"What! Not a thing? But the lamp lights so well!"

He said: "Ah!..." and began to cry.

Surprised, she asked him:

"What's the matter?"

He sobbed:

"I've gone blind!..."

And amidst his tears, he told her in broken sentences everything he'd been feeling for months, how he hadn't worried at the start, then had begun to feel anxiety and horror when he thought of how, soon, everything would disappear for him, and he'd no longer see anything again... never... never!

Then the parade of doctors began. No one knew how to stop the progress of the illness, and soon he was completely blind.

His wife and friends surrounded him with attention

and care. He seemed to have begun a new existence, with the deep inner life of the blind. His emotionless face occasionally lit up in a smile, and one might even say he'd resigned himself.

They made him leave Paris to go live in the country. He liked it there and spent many delightful hours dreaming, lying on a long couch while his wife sat near-by, playing music or reading him poetry. Sometimes he said:

"I'm happy... very happy..."

And when, by chance, he heard her sigh, he looked for her hand, and murmured softly:

"You're here beside me... The ones who truly love me have not abandoned me... I don't miss anything..."

Yet deep in his heart there was an infinite sadness. He remembered the sun from before, and the light he'd once loved so much. He dreamed, despite himself, of a miracle that would restore life to his dull eyes.

One day he was sitting in front of his door when an old woman came up to him:

"Well! My good sir, it's still not getting better?"

"No... It's over now... There's no more hope..."

"And the doctors, what do they say?"

"Nothing... Nonsense..."

"Ah!" said the old woman, "But I know one, an expert, who'll know how to heal you! When my late husband went blind, he went to consult him, seeing as he's so renowned in the country. The doctor said this: 'I promise you nothing, my good man... But... we can try!' 'Oh!' my man said, 'If you make me see, I'll give you half of what I own!' 'I ask for nothing,' said the doctor. 'Come to my hospital.' After two months, yes sir, he did begin to see. Afterward he died suddenly of a congestion, but if he hadn't!... So, you should go..."

76

That very evening, on the peasant woman's advice, he set off, filled with an immense and certain hope that his savior had come.

The doctor examined him at length, then said to him, just as he had to the other:

"I don't promise anything... but I have hope. It will be a long time though, a very long time..."

He cried out:

"What does it matter, if I'm healed!"

When he'd been settled into the convalescent home, he asked:

"May I keep my wife with me?"

"No... Since you'll stay for at least two months in darkness, your wife can't keep you company. What you need is calm, absolute rest. Your wife will visit you every week, and if you wish, we can keep her aware of your condition, day by day."

He said: "Alright," possessed by a sudden fierce selfishness, forgetting everything at the sole idea of regaining his sight.

... When after about three months he was allowed to leave the closed room, he stood for a few seconds without daring to lift his eyelids, delaying the decisive moment in the terror he hadn't been cured. But suddenly his eyes opened, and he let out a great cry:

"I saw!... I can see!..."

Laughing and crying at the same time, he snapped up the blessed day with eager eyes. He still couldn't distinguish anything more than a vague glow. In his night, it was hardly more than a pale and uncertain reflection. Yet he shouted:

"I see!... I want to leave!... Take me home!..."

"Oh!" said the doctor, calming him with a small pat on the shoulder, "Not so fast! This is just when you must be even more careful! Let's not tire ourselves out... For today, that's enough."

He let himself be led away, docile. He stayed up all night, opening and closing his eyes very quickly, just enough to see the light of the night lamp.

When he had recovered a bit from his joy, his first thought was to write his wife. How content she'd be! How happy they'd become now!...

Then an even more exquisite idea came to him! Since he had to stay several weeks still, he wouldn't tell her anything. But one fine day, as if the miracle had occurred suddenly, he'd say to her, very naturally:

"Well! That dress looks good on you!" or: "What a pretty hat you have on!..."

She'd think he was mad, and then he'd throw her backward in a kiss:

"No! I'm not mad! I can see!"

He told the doctor, the nurses, and all those who attended him his idea, and with childish delight instructed them:

"Do you understand? Not a smile, not a word..."

They promised. Little by little he learned to recognize objects again, and to distinguish between beings and faces. He no longer groped; his gestures became precise. Little by little, though, a great impatience also began to take hold of him. He could no longer keep it in.

"Doctor, I'm quite well... Let me go..."

"No... Not yet..."

"When?"

"Soon. For the sake of a few days, you shouldn't risk compromising everything."

But since the wait was making him feverish, and emotional to excess, they let him leave. He'd asked once again that no one be warned. He'd take a car and go to his house, all alone.

On the doorstep, the doctor gave him his last recommendations:

"Remember to come back every week, and above all do not take off your tinted glasses as long as there's sun. The sun is your greatest enemy. If you were to relapse..."

"Oh! Don't be afraid!"

He left.

It was a lovely June morning. He'd folded back the edges of his hat to ensure himself light. The road seemed endless, but at last the first houses of his village appeared. The car crossed the Grande-Rue, and the Market Square. At the bottom of the hill, he told the driver to stop.

"Is this alright?"

"Yes, sir. Look, it's right in front of you."

At the end of the steep path stood the little house, all white, bathed in light, in the blazing garden. The shadows themselves were golden, so gaily did the sun flow down the walls. Since he was very moved, the man's legs trembled slightly beneath him. The heat of approaching midday dazed him, and he climbed the slope slowly. Running his hand between the bars of the gate, he lifted the latch. On tiptoe for fear his footsteps would make the gravel in the garden crunch, he made his way forward. It was so hot that the dog stayed sleeping in his kennel, without hearing him. The shutters were closed. He saw everything for the first time, yet felt at home. He told himself:

"Oh! The pretty, cheerful little house!"

He imagined the interior, the comfortable and cool rooms. He murmured:

"My God, all is well! All is well!"

He was about to call out: "Jeanne! It's me! Come!" But he restrained himself. For the surprise to be complete, he would come up to the door, and when it had opened, he would take her in his arms. He'd dreamed of the moment so often that he could describe it down to the slightest details. And now the dream was becoming reality, a reality bathed in light and joy... just like a dream...!

A bench was leaning against the house, just under a window. As the walk and the emotion had tired him a little, he sat down to catch his breath. Then a murmur of voices came to his ear. Talking, laughing, behind the shutters... he listened... disconnected words... two voices.

"Well!... Who is my wife talking to? Ah! It's my friend Sournize... But what are they saying? They seem very happy... Do they know?..."

He got up and peering through the blinds, looked into the room. The voices stopped, then continued. His wife said:

"Come on, will you be good and go set the table?"

Suddenly he saw them both in a ray of light. She threw her head back, let the washing in her arms fall, abandoned herself laughing in the arms of his friend who kissed her on the neck, the eyes, the lips, long kisses that made her shudder.

He jumped back with a leap, mouth open to scream. Everything seemed to turn around him. With his hand, he looked for the bench, and sank onto it...

Ah! What a horrible, terrible thing! So that's what was in store for his return! While he had endured the torment of going blind, his wife and best friend had been having a good time of it! The wretches! ... They'd known how to lie to his face, mock his empty eyes!...

He rose up, terrifying, fists raised, ready to murder.

But just as he was about to throw himself at the door, he felt his legs give way. The vision of the two years of darkness he'd just lived through, so calm and sweet, so free of doubts, passed before him. And his weakness also appeared to him, his physical and moral fatigue, the feeling that he hadn't been cured, and that a little sooner or a little later, he'd lose his eyes, this time forever! He'd have to live alone then, crazed, like a beast that hides itself to die! This terrifying thought made him freeze... No! No! Anything but that!... Should he have to see those looks not meant for him? Those kisses the traitors would send over his shoulder?... Never!

What prevented him from entering now and pretending to have heard nothing, seen nothing?... He hit himself on the head: I don't want to! I wouldn't know how to pretend. So?...

... Then, as the twelve strokes of noon rose up from the village, and the sun at the height of its arc released a burning light and a furnace of heat, he sat down.

With a slow gesture, he threw off his hat, took off his sunglasses, and opening his eyelids wide, face turned toward the sky, gave up his eyes to be consumed by the sun.

At first there was a glare, then a big red disc flattened over his face... It seemed that something was burning, that everything was against him. He had a moment of revolt. He reached a hand toward his sunglasses... He could no longer see them...

Quiet and calm, the good night, in which all hatreds die, folded itself down on him, like the tired waves that in the low tide of evening come to die on the golden sand of the shores...

The Disappeared

Eight days before, a worker named Gaspard had disappeared. His description was given out to all the public prosecutors. In vain the banks of the Seine were searched, the empty lots where at night the sharp and sinister sounds of prowlers' whistles could be heard, the shanty houses where goons and their girls met to prepare crimes… All that could be learned was that Gaspard had been two months in treatment at the hospital, that he'd been released Monday around noon, and that he'd been seen a few hours later with a stranger at a local cabaret. From that moment on, all trace of him and his companion had been lost. As he had neither money nor jewelry on him, as he was a good laborer, good husband and good father, the investigators found no leads and the case was about to be closed. Then one morning, a man appeared at the station and asked to see the police chief.

"Sir," he said, "you are looking for one Gaspard, who has not appeared at his home for eight days. I can tell you what's become of him, if you'll give me a few minutes of attention. But first it will be necessary to tell you certain things that seem unnecessary, but that I consider essential.

As you see, I am poorly dressed, with stained clothes and a full beard. I'm neither a starving inventor nor the kind of unemployed worker who gets put in prison to find shelter for the winter.

I'm just a medical student, whom bias, malice or a spiteful examiner's nonsense has reduced to poverty.

When I began my studies, my parents were, if not rich, at least well off enough to pay for my needs. One by one, I lost my father and my mother. I found myself alone with all my outstanding accounts, without a friend in the world. But the few bank notes I had, if counted very strictly, would just allow me to take my degree on the condition I acted quickly, not missing a single exam. Once in possession of my title as doctor, I'd have found some remote corner, a position that secured my livelihood temporarily. Everything was calculated well and wisely.

A month ago, I presented myself at my last exam. It was a clinical assessment, one of those considered a simple formality. When you've spent years in the hospital, you have to blunder pretty badly not to pass. But against all expectations, I failed. In front of my examiner, I made a very serious diagnostic error. I did my best to argue, to appeal to my memories, to weigh up all the symptoms and signs, to defend my opinion: it was useless. I was refused. For any other, for myself until a few months before, a failure would have been a small blow to my ego, a delay of a few weeks. In my situation, it took on the proportions of disaster. There were only fifteen francs in my pocket: my whole fortune. Unless gold rained down from the sky, I didn't expect anything else. My friends from the old days had long since left me: I was in absolute, complete distress.

I left the examination room with the conviction that the patient did in fact have what I said, that the teacher was greatly mistaken, and that I, whose analysis had been rejected, was correct! I shut myself away in my room. All night, I pored over notes and medical treatises, and my certainty increased.

The next day, I returned to the hospital. In the

Ambroise-Paré room, bed 27, I saw my man. He was lying down, thin, gaunt, emaciated. His head, from which cheekbones protruded, sank back onto the white pillow. Hair clung, dull and damp, to his moist forehead. His parted lips revealed pale gums and teeth chattering in a constant tremor, while his nostrils flared in quick bursts in his attempt to breathe.

When the patient recognized me, he smiled. I questioned him for a second time. He answered me in the same broken voice I'd heard the day before. Once again I examined him: once again I found the same symptoms. My conviction remained firm.

I thought: it's the other one who's wrong. Yet it was me who had failed. Complain? What good was that! What candidate has ever won a case against his judge?...

Two or three days later I came back, and this time, I left with even more absolute conviction. While I admit the symptoms observed could be interpreted in different ways, the course of the disease itself was giving greater proof to my diagnosis. To tell the truth, the way things were going, my patient would die. Only a miracle could — I won't even say cure him, but extend his life. And my patient was obviously declining, losing his strength: it was a matter of days.

I'm not cruel, I assure you. I cried for my parents, and I never truly recovered from their death. But there, the truth is that I watched the progress of the disease with savage joy, hanging onto this man's agony with genuine pleasure.

Why?... It was no longer with the goal of revising a decision that had stopped my studies, a decision that from now on was final. I was compelled by a dreadful, fierce curiosity. Only children, murderers and scholars have a curiosity like that: and I had become all three at once.

For two days the man gasped. Hoarse sounds came from his mouth; the air rattled in his chest; his fingers pulled the sheets up to his chin with a slow movement — in the countryside they say this is a sign of death. He'd been given his last rites. His neighbors peered at his bed to watch his wheezing. My triumph had come!...

But one morning, when I asked the guard, just as I had every day:

"Well! Number 27?"

He replied:

"They say he's rallying!"

Lying in bed, his face less hollow, his look less fixed, his breathing less suffocated, the man seemed to smile at me. For the first time, I hesitated.

"By any chance, could what he's saying be true?... But no! Impossible!..."

But the next day, and the days following, the improvement continued. The man's fever fell, his appetite returned, the miracle was completed: it was a resurrection.

A fury took hold of me. Despite the apparent clarity of the facts, my doubts at the start had vanished. Against the evidence itself, I remained certain that I was right: he was going to die, it was impossible for him not to die!

That night, I wrangled like a madman between the facts and my conviction. I felt my mind straying... At the window, I thought I could see the sneering, ironic faces of the examiner and the dying man, pressing their noses against the glass to taunt me.

When day came, I ran to the hospital.

"Number 27?"

"Released, this morning."

I nearly fell over backward.

Standing in his rumpled clothes, still thin and weak, but alive, the man stood before me! He said: "Ah! I came back from the dead, didn't I Mister? I won't forget the care you took of me during the last few weeks."

I had to turn away so he wouldn't see the flash in my eyes.

This resurrection became a sort of insoluble problem for me, a living enigma that haunted my days and nights. For a week, I'd eaten almost nothing. The excitement of my brain alone sustained me, and made me go on.

In front of the door of the hospital, I waited:

"Come, my good man, have a drink with me," I said.

He followed me, but refused to let me pay. It would have been impossible anyway, for I didn't have a sou.

"Come to my house," I said to him, "won't you? I'll examine you there at leisure."

"Certainly!"

I was hardly in my room before a horrible thought took hold of me. There, under a few millimeters of skin, bone and muscle, in the lungs of this being, the key to the mystery that haunted me was hidden! Know! I wanted to know! And I could!...

When I leaned my ear against him, I could hear the beating of his heart and the rattle of his short breaths. Near the top of his shoulders, there was a hard blast of air, the kind the opening of big marine shells makes. Behind my closed eyes, I imagined what my ears heard: the collapsed lung, bluish gray, perforated like a beehive, spotted in places with pearl or white colored dots, rough in other parts like a tablecloth with hardened bread crumbs beneath it...

I sat up. With one move, I grabbed a scalpel from

the table, and with a single blow cut his throat.

He fell without a cry.

Then I laid him on the floor, and performed an autopsy on the gasping body.

… Well! Sir, I was right! The man had tuberculosis! By what miracle had he survived?… I don't know. But in the end, that wasn't what I wondered. I was not wrong.

I worked all day and all night for a week. This morning I put the corpse in a trunk. I took it down with the help of my porter, and loaded it into the car waiting outside your door. You'll find it properly stitched up. He's missing nothing but the lungs, which I'll keep.

That is Gaspard, the disappeared man you are searching for. This, sir, is his story and mine.

The Kiss

"Yes, Sister, my poor little one did that for a woman! Ever since he met her, he hasn't been the same any more. He used to be so gentle and polite, but he became nasty and abrupt. He told me lies to avoid giving me his wages on Saturday. Sometimes I waited for him until two in the morning, and when I heard the door close, very slowly, since he knew I'd stay up waiting for him, I'd creep into his room. I saw how his eyes were swollen, how he cried in his sleep.

At first I thought he'd gotten into some trouble at the shop. I went to his boss, and he told me: "Not at all. But we've also noticed that he's disturbed, that he no longer works as well as before. He must have gotten in with bad company." So, taking good care that he didn't notice anything, I watched my boy, and learned he was with a girl from the neighborhood, a hussy, a street girl — excuse me — who at night walks the streets looking for men.

If she'd been a worker like him, even though I'm old and need what he earned to live, I'd have left them together. But her!... I went to go find her. I told her to leave him to me, that I had no one but him. She showed me to the door, insulting me... on the stairs, I heard her scream:

"You want to take him? Well! Just see if I'll give him back to you..."

The next day, they brought me my little boy on a stretcher. A shot in the chest. From what I understood or guessed, he'd begun to argue with her, first on account of me, then because he didn't give her enough money. When he realized she'd amused herself enough, that she didn't want anything more to do with him, without thinking either of himself or me, or anything, he lost his head. You know, he tried to kill himself. Ah! That really brings grief, at my age!"

Standing near the bed of the wounded, the nun listened, without saying a word. The patient, in a coma, breathed with sharp, quick gasps. His mother went on, trembling:

"And what did the doctor say?... Is there hope?"

"It's very serious, my good woman, but you must not despair. He's young... Now, go home. He must not have the excitement of seeing you as soon as he opens his eyes. Don't worry, he'll be well taken care of. You can come a while tomorrow, and every day."

Crying more loudly, but biting her lips so the other beds didn't hear her sobs, the old woman left, turning back at each step to look down the line of identical white beds.

A great silence hung over the room. Night was falling slowly. The noise, the murmurs that had greeted the arrival of a visitor, faded. It was the time that tired patients dozed off. The nun continued to sit at the bedside of the wounded man.

She was very young. Her eyes were clear, and had the amazement of a child. Her mouth still did not bear the wrinkles of those whose lips whisper prayers constantly. Her face was pink and soft, and her hair slipped occasionally from her cap onto her forehead, leaving a golden gleam. But despite her little girl's laugh, she knew the words that could soothe pain. When she spoke to patients, her voice took on the tender inflections of a mother or older sister.

Toward the middle of the night, the wounded man regained consciousness. The Sister hadn't left him. He wanted to question her. She silenced him. He obeyed, docile, and dozed again.

For the first few days, she remained like that, sitting almost ceaselessly near him. He hardly spoke, shy and almost ashamed, and remained motionless for hours, eyes closed, only lifting his eyelids when the door opened and closing them again immediately, to fall back into his torpor.

In those very short moments, once or twice he said, softly:

"Sister..."

And when the Sister, leaning over him, replied:

"What is it, little one?"

Then he collapsed on himself, whispering:

"Nothing... Nothing..."

One morning, he grew bolder:

"Tell me, Sister, since I've been here, has no one come to ask for me?"

"But yes, your mother, didn't you know?"

"Yes... but, besides her?"

"No, no one."

He nodded, and his eyelashes grew moist.

"Come, little one, you must not cry."

But overcome now, after a long silence, he began to speak, out of a great need to confide his sorrow to someone:

"It's not alright... I can tell you everything, you're good to me... and it will be a relief to talk with you... Mother doesn't know, she believes I was wounded by accident... Well! That's not true. I wanted to kill myself..."

90

The Sister stopped him with a gesture:

"She knows..."

"Ah!..."

He went quiet, then nodded:

"My poor old mother!... I've brought her so much grief! She must forgive me... it's not my fault... I was so unhappy. When that woman left me, I thought I couldn't live anymore. I loved her so much!... She did what she wanted with me... And you see, she knows I'm ill, very ill because of her... Even so, she doesn't come to see me. All this time, when I watched the door, and listened to it creak, it was her I was waiting for... I was waiting for her. Now I'm very sure that she won't come... I prefer that... I won't think of her anymore... I no longer love her... No, I do not love her anymore..."

Tears flowed down his cheeks, giving the lie to his words.

He thought, and continued:

"It's a great sin, isn't it, Sister, to want to commit suicide?"

"A very great sin. The greatest."

"When you are too unhappy, though... You who have always prayed to the good Lord, you don't know about that..."

She lowered her head and clasped her hands, her shoulders seemed to shiver, the wings of her cap fluttered, and in a voice so low tears might have been trembling in it, she said:

"Hush... hush... Don't tire yourself... Rest, little one..."

The beginning of the night went well. Then around two o'clock, the patient grew agitated.

"Well!" said the Sister, who had woken. "What is it?... You're restless?"

He replied with incoherent words, stuttering, his voice hard.

She'd taken one of his hands in hers, and with the other wiped his face covered in sweat, trying to calm him.

With this contact, under her slow caress, he grew peaceful. His voice became less sharp, his words stopped running together so much, his meaning became clearer. Occasionally he spoke with an angry tone.

"Ah! You're here? ... But yes. Once again, I arrived too early. I went a bit far to bring you flowers... Not pretty?... Sunday, if you want, we'll go out together. We'll have lunch by the water, and at night we'll turn in early. We'll have all night to love one another... If you knew how much I love you! I love your eyes, your hair, your skin that smells nice."

He said all this in a pleading voice, like a passionate prayer.

Then he began to speak quickly again, blurring his words.

The Sister, her gaze lost, let these phrases go by without interrupting. It was like a music of love, the way his lips mechanically murmured that devotion.

The patient moaned. Suddenly, as he seemed about to doze off, he sat up with a sudden jerk.

"What did you say?... Go away?... Don't come back?..."

He began to pant, his breath short, painful and hoarse, with a rattling sound that startled the nun.

She took a lamp and approached him.

He was pale, with troubled and mad eyes. Long shadows fell over his cheeks to the corners of his lips. His temples seemed to have flattened. His hair, glistening with sweat, stuck in patches to his forehead, and the nostrils of his thin nose flared with his quick breaths, pulling his whole face toward them.

Ah! She knew that face, the face of tormented and terrible agony, as if the soul hoped to relive its whole life in one second...

In a low voice, so as not to disturb the rest of the patients, she told a nurse:

"Quickly... quickly... go find the doctor on shift, the chaplain... Number 6 is not well..."

She kneeled by the bed:

"My God! May your will be done, but forgive this child."

The dying man had taken her hands in his, and was still delirious, but in voice that was distant, distant...

"Stay... I'll give you everything you wish... As long as you don't leave me... If you leave me, I'll die... Come..."

With a slow gesture, he pulled the Sister toward him.

"Come..."

He propped himself up on his elbows:

"Come... come..."

His head brushed the nun's forehead. Neck outstretched, he leaned toward her.

"Come... I adore you..."

He brought his eyes and cheeks closer... He brought his lips to hers.

She shuddered, stiffened and tried to shake him off.

But he took her by the shoulders, and dragging his dream to the threshold of eternity, begged:

"Oh! Stay... I love you..."

... She closed her eyes, and brought her head forward. The dying man took her mouth and bruised it in a silent, deep kiss, one of those intense kisses in which beings mingle, a kiss like those he'd learned in the arms of the prostitute.

In this caress, the Sister's lips were parted and trembling... in a last prayer, or a first thrill?... having lent her virgin flesh, perhaps in memory of a dead love, to this illusion of goodbye.

The 10:50 Fast Train

"What's this, are you leaving us?" the cripple asked me...

"I must. I have to be in Marseille on Monday morning. Tonight, at the Lyon station, I'll take the fast train at 10.50. It's a good train... But you must know it, for if I'm not mistaken, before coming here you were employed at P.L.M.?"

He closed his eyes, and suddenly very pale, whispered:

"Yes... I know it... Oh! Yes!..."

Big tears ran down his cheeks. He went quiet a moment, and continued:

"No one knows it better than me!..."

Believing that only the memory of his former profession had moved him, I said:

"Ah! There's a nice job! It's a smart business!"

He started, and making a violent effort to make his paralyzed body sit up, eyes dry but full of anguish, he protested:

"Oh! Sir! Don't say that! A nice job?... You mean a job of terror and death... A terrifying and nightmarish job... Look... I'm nothing to you, but like you, I... Take the train you like, but not the one at 10.50..."

"Why?" I asked, smiling. "Are you superstitious?"

"I'm not superstitious... I'm just the engineer who operated the Number 17 fast train the day of the catastrophe on 24 July, 1894. And it's such a memory in my life that nothing could ever erase it...

We left from the Lyon station at the usual hour, and drove for about two hours. It was a sweltering day. — On top of the train, despite the considerable speed at which we were traveling, the air hit us in the face, heavy and humid. Real stormy weather, it was…

All of a sudden, as if the knob of an electric lamp had been turned, everything in the sky went out. Except the stars, and the moon, and great bolts of lightning that streaked through the night. They were so clear, so violent and white, that after them the darkness seemed thick as ink.

I said to the other engineer:

"That's it! It's going to rain!"

"About time! I couldn't have put up with this furnace much longer. Pay close attention to the signals."

"Don't worry! I'll keep my eye open!"

The thunder was so loud I couldn't hear the rattling of the wheels or the blast of the locomotive.

The rain still hadn't come but the storm was approaching, and the train was dashing in its direction. One could say we went running after it.

It was nice not to be a coward though. It was something, anyway, to feel oneself launched into the tempest on that steel beast charging like a madman. Before us — oh! not a hundred meters away — a bolt of lightning struck straight into the ground, and it was still blazing before me when one terrible bang reverberated, then another, so harrowing I closed my eyes and fell on my knees.

I remained that way for a few seconds, confused and stunned, in the kind of torpor people must feel after a big blow on the back of the neck.

Finally, I came to. I was still on my knees, with my back against the wall of the cabin. It seemed to me I was returning from hundreds of miles away. I tried to get up. Impossible. My legs remained under me, soft and useless. I thought I'd broken something in my fall. Yet I felt no pain, and I was so light. I wanted to sit up straight, with the help of my hands… but the arms hanging by my sides wouldn't move!

There I was, terrified, with the truly extraordinary feeling that my arms and legs were no longer mine, that I no longer was in command of them… or that they didn't want to obey me… that they were lifeless things, like my clothes the wind lifted… I don't know what feeling or force stopped me from opening my eyes.

We were driving at full speed. The storm roared again, but less harshly, more distant. The rain fell. I heard it splatter on the steel, and felt the warm drops on my face.

A great peace filled me. I felt completely well, really, just a bit tired. But the memory of my profession, my work, woke me up. I still didn't understand what strange phenomenon had me paralyzed, but I called my driver to help me:

No answer!

The speeding engine made a deafening noise. I called out, louder.

"François! Hey, François! Give me a hand!…"

Nothing! Then anxiety overcame me. I was afraid. Afraid of who? Of what?… I didn't know… I opened my eyes and let out a yell. Yes, I must have screamed with fright.

The cabin was empty. The other engineer had disappeared!

In that second, with surprising speed and clarity, everything that had happened since the thunderbolt appeared to me.

Lightning had struck us, killing the driver and throwing him on the track. As for me, I was paralyzed!...

No, sir, even if I were a scholar and had words and more words to choose from, none in the world would give you an idea of the terror that gripped me.

In the heat of battle, soldiers see their comrades fall around them, and yet remain at their posts, weapon in hand. But at least they know where the blow striking them is coming from! They can look at a collapsed body. They fear a bullet, yet they expect it. My companion was taken from me as if by magic, ripped away!... Vanished!...

That's not all. This first vision had hardly clarified, before another rose up, so terrible that I can't recall it without a shudder.

Behind me, in the railway wagons, two hundred travelers were sleeping or talking peacefully; two hundred human beings were swept up in a dizzying rush; two hundred were hurtling toward death, for they had no one to drive them but an inert and impotent thing, incapable of even stretching out an arm, a paralytic... a cripple... me!...

And while my body was incapable of acting, my thought could juggle visions, memories.

First, the shape of the line appeared to me. Before me, I saw the rails shine under the light of the moon. We were hurtling on! And on!... Ah! I rediscovered the exhilaration of speed that habit makes you forget! The train went like lightning through a small station. Its course was so dizzying that I hardly had time to make out an office on the platform, an employee sleeping near a telegraph instrument. One or two vibrations on the hub; the slamming of discs; intersecting rails barring the way, which was suddenly wider then more constricted... a deep trench, then again, the rush through the night...

After that came the tunnel we dove into with the force of a hurricane... and once again the way was open. Now, because I knew where we were, I thought:

"This time, we'll derail. In two minutes we come to a curve so sharp that at this pace, our wheels will swerve off the tracks..."

Once again the good Lord clearly didn't want that to happen. The engine, the whole train leaned... the rails squealed under the crazed wheels... and we made it!...

That railing had been my great terror. I breathed. If the fires weren't fed they'd burn out... The engine would stop... The station guard would run alongside the train... I'd tell him what had happened... He'd place warning signs in front and behind... We were saved!...

But my calm didn't last long! We'd just burned through a station, when I saw something that made my hair stand on end: the disc was closed. The track we were headed toward was not free...

From that moment, I don't know how I didn't go mad. Imagine what can happen in the brain of a man who, trapped on a locomotive at more than a hundred kilometers per hour, is notified that an obstacle will block the route!...

Nothing existed for me but this thought:

"If you don't stop, you'll crush yourself and your whole train! — Avoiding this disaster would require just one gesture! The simple act of grabbing the levers fifty centimeters away... But you won't make this gesture. You can't do it... and you'll see everything... you'll witness the drama... you'll live this agony a hundred times worse than death, because you'll see in front of you the thing that will crush you... you'll see it grow

99

larger... and then rush onto it!..."

I wanted to close my eyes... I couldn't. Some force was stronger than me, stronger than anything... And I saw it, yes, sir, I saw it! I guessed the obstacle before it appeared. Then I had no doubt... It was a train in distress blocking the way. I could make out its shadows and rear lights! It was coming closer... closer... I yelled: "Help! Stop!..." But who could hear me? My train barreled forward. Everything had died in me, except my mind. With my mind I lived the horrifying sights of my eyes in the night, my ears that could hear all sounds above the hum of the wheels, my will that threw me frantic orders like a captain trying to gather his defeated soldiers.

It was coming closer!... Five hundred meters... three hundred... shadows ran over the rails... one hundred... one hundred meters, that's to say a flash!... This was the end!... The meeting... the grave... the crush!...

Ah! Sir! If you haven't seen that!...

... I came to under a pile of steel and rubble. Terrible cries could be heard in the night. In the field, I could see people running, carrying lanterns, while others lifted the wounded in their arms... those screams... that crying...

I saw and heard it all. I didn't suffer. I didn't think... I didn't call out for help...

Between two steel beams that crossed over my head, so close that my lips brushed against them, I just looked at a tiny patch of sky, so gentle, so pure, where a tiny star trembled, clear and beautiful... it laughed...

Illusion

Pale with cold, clutching at the few sous in the bottom of his pockets, which he'd collected from a morning of opening and closing doors, head leaning on his shoulder, trying to escape the wind, the beggar wandered through the crowd, too tired to ask for pity from passersby, too frozen to stretch out his bare hand.

The snow came down in small slanting flakes that clung to his beard, and melted on his neck. Without even noticing it, he thought:

"If I were rich for an hour... — I'd like a car!..."

He paused, reflected a bit, nodded and said to himself:

"And after that?..."

He went on with his dream. Yet as soon as he'd formulated it, he shrugged his shoulders.

"That's not how it is! It's so difficult to find a moment of true happiness..."

... As he was thinking this, he saw, on the porch of a house, another beggar who was shivering, his face drawn, his hand outstretched, asking in a voice so sad and weak it was lost in the murmur of the street:

"Alms, please... Alms..."

Beside the beggar, there was a dog sitting, a poor dog with wet fur, numb with cold, trembling on its feet, whimpering very softly and wagging its tail. He stopped. The dog, beside its companion in misery, barked more loudly and rubbed its nose against him.

He looked at the beggar, his rags, his worn-out

shoes, his hands blue with cold, his impassive face, deathly pale and with closed eyes, the gray sign hanging from his chest, bearing the word: "Blind".

The blind man, feeling a man near him, repeated his pathetic refrain:

"Have pity, sir... Alms..."

The beggar remained motionless. Passersby hurried on their way, heads turned. A woman wrapped in furs, followed by a liveried footmen who opened her umbrella, made her way through the passageway, walking quickly on tiptoe, covering her mouth with her sleeve, before jumping into a car.

The blind man kept murmuring in his monotone voice:

"Alms... Please..."

But no one paid him any attention. Then, the beggar took a few sous from his pocket and held them out to him. Seeing his gesture, the dog barked with pleasure. The blind man closed his trembling hands on the coins and said:

"Thank you, sir... The good Lord will reward you..."

When he heard the word "sir", the beggar was about to exclaim:

"No! Not sir, my poor old man! It's a wretch like yourself in front of you..."

But he remained silent, and knowing how to talk to the poor, replied:

"No need to thank me, my good man..."

"You're very kind, sir... It's so cold, and you took your hand from your pocket to give to me. This season is not kind to the ill!... If only you knew!..."

An immense pity filled the heart of the beggar, who murmured:

"I know... I know..."

Then, forgetting his own misfortune in front of this unfortunate man, he asked:

"Have you been blind since birth?"

"No... it's come with the years... at Quinze-Vingts, the hospital for the blind, they told me I had an illness of old age... a cataract, they called it, I think... but I know, I do, that it's not just old age that put it there!... It's suffering, crying... I've cried so much..."

"Have you been so misfortunate?"

The blind man clasped his hands:

"Oh! Sir!... In the space of a year, I lost my wife, my daughter, my two sons... all those I loved... all those who loved me... I almost died myself, then was healed... But I couldn't work anymore... so poverty came... a great poverty... I don't eat every day, you know!... I haven't had anything since yesterday but a piece of bread, and I gave half to my dog... but with this you've given me, I'll can buy a little for tonight and to-morrow." While listening, the beggar felt the sous at the bottom of his pocket. He sorted them with his fingers, distinguishing with his touch the big from the small. He counted out twenty-three. Then he said:

"Come with me. It's too cold here. I'm going to take you to eat something."

The blind man blushed with pleasure, and stammered:

"Oh! Sir, you're too kind..."

"Come..."

He took him by the arm, making sure not to brush against him, as he didn't want the other to feel his damp, overly light clothing. Then they set off. The dog, nose to the wind, ears perked up, attentive, wove between people, pulling brusquely on the leash when they went through the area with cars. They walked for a long time, then stopped in front a small restaurant on a dark street.

The beggar opened the door, and said to the blind man:

"Come in…"

Then, after finding a table near the stove, he showed the man to a chair, and sat by him. Around them, silent workers ate from small heavy plates. The blind man, after taking the leash off his dog, stretched his hands toward the fire, and sighed:

"It's good here…"

The beggar called the girl who was serving and said:

"Soup and boiled meat."

The girl asked:

"And for you?…"

"Nothing."

When the soup, which had a rich smell of vegetables and meat, was before him, the blind man slowly began to eat, without speaking. The beggar looked at him closely, while cutting small pieces of bread he fed to the dog under the table. Once the soup and meat were finished, he said:

"Drink a glass, it'll give you legs!"

He called the serving girl:

"How much?"

"One franc five."

He paid, leaving two sous as tip, and helped up his companion.

When they were in the street again, he asked:

"Is it far, where you're staying?"

"Where are we?"

"Near the Saint-Lazare station."

"A fair way then… I sleep in a warehouse on the

other side of the water."

"Well! I'll take you a bit of the way."

The blind man thanked him again. He replied:

"No... no... there's no need..."

Without being able to explain to himself why, he felt happy, deeply happy, more than he had ever remembered being. He walked, lost in a dream, forgetting he hadn't eaten since the day before either and didn't have a place to sleep, forgetting his poverty and rags, forgetting he was a beggar. From time to time he said to the blind man, gently:

"I'm not going too fast, am I?... You're not too tired?..."

The blind man, humble and grateful, replied:

"No... oh! No, sir!..."

And he smiled to be called that, lulled by this illusion he'd given another, and that this other had given him, that he was a happy man, a charitable rich man...

On the docks, feeling the cool breeze off the nearby water, the blind man told him:

"Now I can find my way alone. I have my dog."

"Yes, I'll leave you," said the beggar, sounding serious.

For he'd had a strange thought: Hadn't the mirage he'd so fervently and frequently desired just happened? For a few moments, hadn't he had the illusion of happiness?... Hadn't the path traveled beside this humble man offered him what the luxury, good food and love of his imagination had not?... Wasn't it true that this blind man had no idea he was leaning on the arm of a beggar just like him? Hadn't he himself felt rich, and would he ever recover such a profound, unadulterated joy again, the kind he'd felt on this night?...

While he was thinking, something disturbed his

dream. Reality returned. He said a second time:

"Yes… I'll leave you."

They'd reached the middle of the bridge. He stopped, and fumbled in his pockets to see if he couldn't find a few sous… But nothing…

Then he took the hand of the blind man and squeezed it a long time, as the other said:

"Thank you, sir… Tell me your name, so I can repeat it in my prayers…"

He murmured to him, very softly:

"It's not important… Go back now… You've made me very happy… Goodbye…"

He took a few steps, stopped, stared fixedly at the water shivering before him, said again in a louder voice:

"Goodbye…"

And suddenly he climbed over the parapet…

… a loud splash of water… calls: "Help!… Run to the bank!"

The blind man, unmoving, jostled by people running past, cried out:

"What is it?… What's the matter?…"

A child who'd almost knocked him over when colliding with him, answered without stopping:

"A tramp's gone for a dip!"

With a weary gesture, the blind man shrugged and murmured:

"At least he had the courage, that one!…"

Then, he touched the side of his dog with his foot and set off again, feeling the ground with his stick, face turned toward the sky, bent over at the waist… not knowing…

A Learned Man

Nadal, the great Nadal, a professor at the Faculty of Medicine, a member of the Institute and a grand officer of the Legion of Honor, was going to die.

For forty years he had been the glory and pride of his profession. The son of workers, by virtue of his work alone, he'd achieved the highest honors. Even the most rigorous bowed before his scientific integrity, the poorest before his inexhaustible goodness. He could have been a millionaire, but lived modestly in an apartment on the Left Bank. Whatever the weather, summer or winter, he'd go walking through the popular neighborhoods, to sit at the bedside of the most humble.

A noble character was disappearing, one of those rare specimens of humanity that merely by existing, serve as consolation for all the ugly aspects of life. He had been a learned and wise man, and his end had the quiet harmony of a beautiful evening.

When he felt death coming, he called his favorite students to his side.

When they had gathered around his bed, he made a gesture for them to come near. Then, with his body bent forward and his arms stretched out, fingers clinging to the blanket, he remained silent a few moments.

Great shadows fell from his large forehead onto his pale face.

In the corner, an old man was weeping in silence. The others, looking thoughtful, did not make a sound.

He opened his eyes, and in that deep, serious voice

known so well to the poor he'd comforted and the fol-
lowers whose minds he'd shaped, he spoke:

"Dear friends, I thank you deeply for coming to
hear the final words of your former teacher, who is leaving you now."

He paused, searching for the way to continue. His
voice, so clear and vivid, seemed deafening. The sentences that had once tumbled from his lips, strong and
precise images, now fled from him.

One of his students said very softly:

"Teacher, you should not tire yourself..."

He lifted his head, pressed his fingers to his temples
and spoke again:

"I am not tired... It is not death that muffles my
voice and prevents me from speaking... no... it is fear!.."

All of them, heating him say a word he had never
said before, looked at one another, dumbfounded.

He went on:

"Yes... fear... fear of what I'm going to tell you, for
it's such a frightening thing that my hair bristles at the
mere thought of revealing it to you, and you'll be frozen
with terror once you've heard it!

Come closer... I'll tell you my whole life... the
crime I will atone for...

I've seen murderers... I've seen parricides... But it's
not one of the infamous criminals I tremble to meet with
again down there...

Listen to me...

All of you are here because you took part in my
work, the research to which I dedicated my life. You
know the wild obstinacy with which I worked to discov-
er the nature of cancer, its treatment, its cure... I spent
days and nights leaning over cultures, shut away in my
laboratory. I knew all the torments of inventors... you

suffered them with me. Then one fine day, with all our work, calculations and assays we arrived at a result... remember... I made the first application of my serum.

I asked you to swear not to breathe a world to any living soul. God is my witness that I had no criminal intent at that time. I simply wanted to be able to continue my tests with calm and contemplation. You didn't know the subject I was experimenting on, and none of you tried to find out..."

He took his head in his hands, pressing on his eyes as if to crush a passing vision, then continued in a loud voice:

"Well! The patient I treated was cured!

At first, I believed it was a simple coincidence, and hesitated to tell you about it. So I tried a second experiment, a third... ten... twenty... thirty! All were successful!

As I hadn't told the patients, neither they nor those close to them affected by their illness could spread word of the marvelous cure. I was alone in the world, alone in the knowledge of that incredible thing I'd discovered!..."

For the second time, he paused, then sighed:

"It was dreadful!

Any other, in my place, would have been euphoric with joy. A pride without limits would have flooded his heart... Not me!

An extraordinary thing happened to me... it seemed an immense void was coming to make a hollow in my life, and that suddenly everything I made my goal, my motive, had vanished!

Consider that for thirty years, all my days and all my sleepless nights had been haunted by this one problem: the cure for cancer! And suddenly, in one moment, my thought no longer had anything to cling to, my activity had no field where it could exert itself!

I'd followed that terrible evil just as a patient gardener follows the bud on which leaves gradually begin to be glimpsed. I admit I'd sympathized with the sufferings of men, but — I fully realize it now — the disease interested me far more than the patients.

What a horrible thing! I felt more pleasure, more delight, in studying the plague than fighting it!...

Now it had ended. Those carefree hours, when I'd worked as a poet does following a dream, had vanished. Instead of the considerations of each day, I felt the anguish of each second; instead of the feeling of joy with which you follow a horse galloping down a racetrack with your fortune, instead of that... a few cubic centimeters of liquid under the skin, and a quick cure... it was idiotic!...

You don't dare look at me! You turn your heads... But you still don't know everything, and I want to tell you everything."

His voice faltered, and his forehead was covered with sweat. He called out: "Drink!" and emptied in one go the glass of water handed to him. He wiped his lips on the back of his sleeve and went on, speaking quickly:

"I'm hurrying, for I must arrive at the end. All of you here remember that day I told you sadly: Our experiment did not work... Nothing even close to a result... Everything must be redone. You believed me. You did not complain, and I lied! And here comes the most terrible part of my terrible crime."

He turned his head slowly toward the old man, who'd just begun to cry in silence.

"Listen, Dornoy, come here, come close... That was when your wife was dying of cancer... your wife, the beloved companion of your life... the one who stayed by you, smiling through the hardest trials, the one you cherished above all... There was an evening I saw you at home, in this bedroom, sobbing because you knew you would lose her, and you said:

"Why have I learned so much, if all I can take from today is the certainty that no power on earth knows how to save her!"

As I listened to you, evil thoughts came to me. I had that superhuman power, I had it!... But the evil voice, the hideous voice of relentless scientific curiosity, screamed so loudly in my ears that I no longer understood my own conscience. I struggled, all the same. I was on the verge of crying out: "Look! Here it is! Take it! Your wife is saved!..." You whispered: "Give me your serum... so I know I've tried everything..." And suddenly I felt like I'd turned to marble. Not a fiber in my heart quivered, and I answered you: "What good would that do?... It would only increase her suffering!..."

You left, and when the door had closed, I ran to my laboratory, and to make sure I wouldn't succumb to temptation, I shattered my test tubes... I destroyed the cultures... I tore up all my papers, so that while I was alive, no one else would be able to trace my discovery... and my crime. Sure at last that my secret was hidden from all, that from then on I'd still be able to follow the hideous evil and track its movements, I took up my investigations again, on other bases... once more I was separated from the world by the selfish intoxication of research!

But — and this was the beginning of my atonement — I always returned to my starting point. I always saw before me that which I thought I'd torn up, but that I hadn't destroyed at all, for my thought could no longer separate from it. Research had no more charm for me, since no sooner had the problem been posed, then I had the solution...

For the first time in my life, I had to stop all work!"

He took a moment, seeking to regain control of his breathing, which had become wheezing and shallow:

"That is my crime, the most appalling one possible, for it is a crime against all humanity.

For my punishment to be complete, you must know what the cure was. You will publish it. But I beg you, I order you not to put my name on it. I do not deserve that honor."

He was suffocating. Someone wanted to sit him up in bed. He pushed the help away, and with twisted features, eyes fixed, he gasped with such authority that all obeyed him:

"Write it down! The manufacture of my serum is based on the fact that a solution..."

He suddenly jerked backward, mouth wide open, face ashen. Gradually he slid down onto the pillows, and hands clutching the sheet, a shudder passed through him...

... Then, the one who had cried earlier, the one whose wife he had let die, leaned over him, put his fingers on his empty eyes, closed his eyelids, and in a soft voice that had no anger in it but trembled a bit, said to the others:

"It's over... You go now... I'll stay with him..."

"Blue Eyes"

Wearing the big hospital gown that made her look even thinner, the little patient stood unmoving by the foot of her bed.

She had sharp features, with blue eyes so big they lit up her whole face: sorrowful eyes, that were deep and outlined. On her pale cheeks, both touched with red, a line descended, the path traced by her tears. When the young doctor stopped before her, she raised her head.

"Well! Little Number Four, what did you say? You want to leave?"

She replied, in a very low voice: "Yes, sir…"

"It's not reasonable. You've only just gotten up after eight days! With this weather, you'll fall ill again. Wait a while. You aren't unhappy here, are you?… No one's giving you a hard time?"

In the same humble and very sweet tone, she replied again:

"No… Oh! No, sir…"

"Then?…"

This time, with a little more energy in her voice, she said:

"I need to go out."

And speaking quickly, anticipating the question, she went on:

"Today is All Saints' Day. I promised to bring flowers to my friend's grave… I swore… He had no one else… If I don't go there, no one will… I swore…"

A tear gleamed in her eye. She brushed it away with

a finger.

Perhaps because he was moved by this terrible pain, perhaps out of curiosity, perhaps mechanically, or perhaps so as not to remain silent and go without a word of pity, the doctor asked:

"Has he been dead a long time?"

"Soon it will be a year..."

"Of what? Do you know?"

Suddenly she looked even smaller, her shoulders more hunched, her hands more pale, her eyes half-closed, her lips trembling. She whispered: "He was executed..."

The doctor bit his lips, and said very quietly:

"Oh! I'm sorry, my poor little one. Since you insist, you may go... Don't catch a cold. And come back tomorrow."

... When the metal gate of the hospital shut behind her, she shuddered.

It was a desolate autumn morning, and rain trickled down the walls. Everything was gray: the sky, the houses, the bare trees and the hazy horizon toward which people walked quickly, fleeing the sadness of the streets. As she'd fallen ill in the middle of summer, she was wearing only a very thin skirt and light camisole. The crumpled ribbon she wore around her scrawny neck made her look even more pathetic.

A skirt, blouse and ribbon that would smile in the sun, seemed to cry on this bleak day... She began to walk with an uncertain step, stopping every minute, breathless, with a heavy head. All those who passed would turn around for a few seconds. She seemed to hesitate, ready to speak, then, fearful, looking right and left, continued on her way...

She crossed half of Paris that way. On the docks,

she remained unmoving, contemplating the heavy, muddy tide. A great cold shook her, and fearing she would not be able to go on, she started off again.

At Maubert Square, passing Gobelins Avenue, she felt almost home, in her neighborhood. Soon she met with familiar faces, people who when they saw her pass, said:

"But... isn't that Vandat's mistress?... How she's changed!..."

"Which Vandat?"

"But of course, Vandat the kill—..."

She quickened her step, covering her ears with her hands so as not to hear the end of the word... Day was ending when she arrived at the run-down hotel, where she'd lived before her illness.

She went in. Pimps and girls were playing cards in the small downstairs café. As soon as they saw her, they cried out:

"Hey, look! It's 'Blue Eyes'!" (She'd used to go by that name.) "Will you have anything, 'Blue Eyes'? Sit down..." Moved, and suffocated by the thick and bitter smoke in the air, she coughed, suddenly very red. Then she answered:

"No... I don't have time... Is the Madame here?"

"Yes, there she is."

She smiled shyly:

"Madame, I'm here for some clothes. I'm a little cold with just these ones on..."

"We had to move your old things up to the attic. I'm not sure exactly where they are. Until we find them, stay here to warm up."

"No, I don't have time... I'll come back later."

She made her way toward the door. A man sneered:

"Already back to work? You don't waste time!"

115

She went out. The cold now seemed to her even more biting, after spending time in that overly heated room. People passed on the sidewalk, holding bouquets of flowers and wreaths. Those in mourning walked slowly. Others also carried bouquets and wore their Sunday best, but chatted and laughed, going to the cemetery without great emotion, as if fulfilling a duty out of custom more than feeling.

Without being related to those men, women and children, it was easy to guess who had been touched most closely by the death, and who had their own funerals approaching.

Along the road, small carts were stopped, selling flowers. Chrysanthemums with drooping petals leaned in bunches over roses, and here and there mimosas let their gold powder fall on violets. Closer to the cemetery, in front of the marble, flowerpots were lined up, sad and all looking the same: common spindle flowers with dark leaves, pansies with petals that looked like anxious faces, and farther on, perennials and large pearly garlands…

She looked at all this with an envious eye, thinking:

"If only I could take something to him!… There in the back of the cemetery, in that poor deserted patch, he rests without a cross, without a word!"

"Killer!"

She hardly thought of that! He was the man she loved, her lover, the one who had been there, the lover who had possessed her body, her whole soul…

In a moment of madness, he had killed…

Hadn't he paid his horrible debt?… From the day he'd been taken away, she'd sworn never to be with another again, to leave her life of a lost girl, to work and become honest, to be forgotten… Just remembering him wasn't enough!…

She kept looking at the flowers. The seller asked:

"A bouquet? Chrysanthemums? Roses?…"

She went away without answering, for she didn't have a sou.

Then an idea lodged itself in her head: "Flowers, I need flowers… I must give them to him… I swore I would."

She was collapsing from fatigue and hunger, but hardly thought of it. She thought of nothing else but the bare ground where he was buried, which a humble bouquet would cheer up for a few hours… Yes, but the money!…

Naturally, an idea came to her, and after her vow of honesty it no longer upset her. Like a good laborer who returns to his shop to take up his tools and work, after tying up her hair into a bun and smoothing her blouse with a mechanical gesture, she began to walk along the roads. So many times, while her man was playing at the cabaret, she'd prowled the night there, making her living with neither sadness nor joy…

She walked back and forth, looking about her, swaying her hips, provocative, whistling at men between her teeth: "Psstt!… Listen up…" All of them hurried on, seeing how skinny she looked. Her ravaged face was no longer truly made for pleasure, nor was her gaunt body or chest, with its shoulders sticking out from her too light camisole.

Before, when she'd been pretty, when she was "Blue Eyes", she'd never been without a client for long. But now!…

"Psstt!… Listen up!… Psstt! Handsome blonde…"

All of them passed, without turning their heads. The daylight was disappearing. As she strode along the pavement, she thought:

"It's going to close before I can buy flowers…"

A mist was descending silently, which could hardly be felt. The shapes of things had begun to dissolve in shadow. In her starved figure, little more than her eyes could be made out, her eyes gleaming with pain.

A man turned the corner of a deserted street, his coat collar turned up, hands in his pockets. She brushed past him, and murmured in her husky voice, putting all the strength of her desire into it:

"Listen… Come with me…"

He looked at her a moment. She'd approached him, sinking her gaze into his, her infinite gaze that was no longer the hopeful look of a girl. He took her arm.

She led him to the seedy hotel she'd visited earlier. Quickly, half opening the door, she said:

"My key… A candle…"

The Madame whispered to her softly:

"In 23, second floor, third door."

She said, all the same: "I know…"

The men and girls leaned toward one another. While going up the stairs, she heard their exclamations and laughter.

… When she came down, it was almost night. She said a quick "goodbye" to her momentary companion and began to run. She stopped at the flower seller, picked a bouquet at random and tossed him two half-note coins, which clinked in his hand.

Quickly, quickly, she walked toward the cemetery. People were leaving in groups. She trembled:

"I hope I arrive in time!…"

Behind the door, a guard told her: "Too late. We're closed!"

She begged:

"Oh! Sir! Time to go in and out… two seconds…"

"Go then, but fast."

She ran over the walkways, stumbling over the stones. The path was long. She breathed with difficulty, with a burning feeling in her chest. At the Wall of the Tortured, she stopped, fell on her knees and scattered flowers on the ground. Big tears rolled down her cheeks, onto the palms of her hands where she hid her face. She tried to pray, but she didn't know any prayers, and pressing her lips to the earth, she sobbed:

"Oh! My little one! My little one!…"

Then, tired, so tired she no longer felt her legs, but with a bit of joy in her heart, she rose and went out. She smiled at the guard: "You see, I wasn't long."

Now that she'd visited her man, she became aware of her fatigue and cold. She dragged herself along, coughing, leaning against the walls.

She got to the hotel, and opened the door. In the living room, smoky and too hot, girls and pimps were playing cards. She stood motionless in the doorway and said: "Good afternoon." The conversation went silent. She tried to laugh. A woman leaned back in her chair and shouted: "Say, 'Blue Eyes'! You put on a pretty show for your return!…"

She shrugged. The other went on: "You don't know who that was?"

"No…" "Well! It was the Hangman!"

"Blue Eyes" stammered:

"What did you say? The..."

And the girl, taking a drink and making her move in the game, shouted: "The Hangman… The executioner, how about that!…"

The Debt Collector

Ravenot, a debt collector for ten years at the same bank, was a model employee. There had never been the slightest complaint against him, never the slightest error noted in his accounts.

Living alone, carefully avoiding new relationships, not visiting the café, without a mistress, he seemed happy and free of desires. If on occasion someone said to him:

"It must be tempting to handle such large sums!"

He simply replied:

"Why? Money that doesn't belong to you isn't money."

He was the honest man in his neighborhood, the referee on sensitive issues.

Then, one deadline night, he didn't return home. The idea of a criminal act on his part never even crossed the mind of those who knew him. The hypothesis of crime was only possible. The police confirmed his round. He had punctually presented his tickets and cashed his final value by the gate of Montrouge around seven. His revenue therefore amounted to over two hundred thousand francs. After that, they'd lost his trail. They made raids on the wasteland around the fortifications and conducted a search of the squalid shacks dotted here and there about the military zone: Nothing. To set their minds at ease, they telegraphed in all directions to the frontier stations. But for the directors of the bank, just as much as for security, there was no doubt that prowlers had followed Ravenot, robbed him and thrown him in the river. On the basis of certain indications, they even believed that they could claim the exploit had been prepared for a long time by professional criminals.

Only one man in Paris shrugged when he read this in the newspapers: Ravenot.

Once the cleverest sleuths at police headquarters had lost his trail, he'd come to the Seine by the outer boulevards. Under the arch of a bridge, he'd taken the bourgeois clothing left there the day before, put the two hundred thousand francs cashed in his pockets, made his uniform and bag into a weighted bundle like an enormous stone, thrown everything in the river and calmly returned to Paris. He spent the night at a hotel and slept peacefully. In just a few hours, he had become a skilful thief.

Taking advantage of his lead, he might have been able to take the train and cross the border. But he was too shrewd to believe a few hundred kilometers would shelter him from the police, and had no illusions about the fate awaiting him. He would be caught; there was no doubt in that regard. And so his reasoning went in another direction.

When day came, he slipped the two hundred thousand francs in an envelope on which he fixed five stamps, then went to a notary.

"Sir," he said, "here's the thing. I have some investments in this envelope, some papers I wish to keep safe. I'm leaving on a long journey, and don't know when I'll get back. So I'm going to trust you with it. There's no objection, I assume, to this deposit?"

"None. I'll write you a receipt..."

He agreed, then thought it over. A receipt? But where would he put it? To whom could he entrust it? If I keep it on me, I'll lose all the benefit of my deposit...

He hesitated, not having foreseen this complication, then said very naturally:

"My God, I am alone in the world, with no parents, no friends. The journey I am undertaking is very... dangerous. My receipt runs the risk of being lost... destroyed... To make sure things go smoothly — who knows if I'll live or die — couldn't you keep this paper in your archives? That way, when I return, it'll be enough to say my name, either to you, or your successor...."

"The problem is...."

"You may note on the receipt it cannot be reclaimed in any other way. If that entails a risk, I am the only one to run it."

"Agreed! Please tell me your name."

He answered without hesitation:

"Duverger, Henri Duverger."

Once he was in the street, he breathed a sigh of relief. The first part of his program had been completed. He put his hand on his collar: the product of his theft was now out of reach.

He'd calculated coldly: When my term expires, I'll collect my deposit. No one will be able to challenge me in my property. Four or five bad years have to pass, then I'll be rich. It's less stupid than slaving away all my life! I'll go live in the country. I'll be Monsieur Duverger to everyone. I'll grow old calmly, an honest man doing good, without remorse.

He waited another twenty-four hours to be sure the numbers on the bank notes hadn't been traced. Then, reassured on this point, cigarette between his lips, he deliberately went to give himself up as prisoner.

Another, in his place, would have imagined some

story. He preferred to tell the truth, and confess his theft. What good was it to waste time? But neither during the inquiry nor at the criminal court could any word be dragged out of him concerning the location of the 200,000 francs. All he said was:

"I don't know anymore. I fell asleep on a bench... I was robbed too."

With his impeccable record, he was condemned to only five years in prison. He welcomed the arrest without batting an eye. He was thirty-five years old. At forty, he'd be free and rich. He considered this a minor, necessary sacrifice.

At the central prison where he served his sentence, he was a model inmate, just as he'd been a model employee. He passed the days without impatience or excitement, worried only about his health.... And at last, the day of his liberation arrived! His tiny savings were returned to him, but he wanted to go immediately to the notary.

He'd dreamed of this hour so long! In his head, he saw the scene just as it was going to happen:

He arrived, and was shown into the great solemn office. Didn't the notary recognize him? He looked at himself in a mirror. It's true that he'd aged, that his face was now ravaged... No, the notary certainly did not recognize him. Ha! Ha! This would only be funnier!

"What can I do for you, sir?"

"I've come for a deposit made with you five years ago."

"What deposit...? In what name?"

"In the name of Mister...."

He stopped suddenly, and murmured:

"Well, that's strange...! I can't remember the name I gave!"

He searched and searched for it.... Nothing! He sat on a bench, and with a growing irritation, said to himself:

"Come now... calm...! Mister.... Mister.... It started with... what letter...?"

For an hour, he turned his memory over and over, trying to find a landmark, a hint.... Wasted effort. The name was dancing in front of him, around him; he could see the letters jump, the syllables flee.... Every second he had the feeling of having it before his eyes, on his tongue.... No! First it had been no more than an annoyance; then, it had become infuriating, exasperating... precise, painful, almost physically...! Waves of heat rose from his kidneys to his neck. His muscles twitched, and he couldn't remain in place. Tics shook his hands. He bit his dry lips. He wanted to cry and fight at the same time. But the more he concentrated his attention, the more the name seemed to dance away from him. He stamped his foot, stood up and said:

"What good is it to look for it...? I won't find it. I just have to stop thinking about it, and it'll come to me on its own!"

But you can't strike an obsessive idea just like that from your head. He could stare at the passersby all he liked, and see without seeing; he could listen to the sounds of the street, and hear without hearing. A single question persisted:

"Mister...? Mister...?"

Night came. The sidewalks became deserts. Exhausted with fatigue, he went into a hotel, asked for a room and threw himself fully dressed into bed. He was still searching. At dawn he fell asleep. When he woke, it was broad daylight. He stretched out, satisfied, before the satisfaction flew off all of a sudden, as the question returned:

"Mister…? Mister…?"

A new feeling was added to his anxiety: Fear! The fear of never finding the name again. He got up, went out and walked around for hours, wherever his feet took him, circling the house of the notary. For the second time, night fell. He dug his nails into his skull, moaning:

"It's enough to make you go mad!"

A frightening idea came to him. He had 200,000 francs in banknotes, 200,000 francs — ill-gotten, yes, but belonging to him — and there was no way to get hold of them! He'd spent five years in jail, and now they were escaping! They were within reach, with just one word, a simple word that didn't want to come, and that would make him lose it all! He struck his head with great blows, feeling his reason giving way. He collided with the gas lamps, stumbled down the street like a drunk, crashed into the curbs of the sidewalks. It was no longer simply an obsession, a pain. It was a frenzy of his whole being, his brain and flesh! He was sure he'd never again find it. It seemed a voice was sneering in his ears, that passersby were laughing at him. He began to run straight ahead, jostling people, not even avoiding cars. He would have liked someone to raise a hand against him, so he could hit him in turn; for a horse to roll him on the ground and trample on his flesh….

"Mister…? Mister…?"

At his feet, the Seine flowed murkily, glittering under the stars. He sobbed:

"Mister...? Oh! That name!... That name!..."

He descended the steps that led to the bank. Lying on his belly, he reached toward the river, to cool his hands and face there. He gasped…; water pulled him in… took his eyes… his ears… his whole body…. He felt himself slipping, did not even make a gesture to cling to the embankment... and fell.... The cold stung him. He struggled... reached out his arms... raised his head... disappeared... bobbed to the surface, and suddenly, in a desperate effort, eyes terrified, he shouted:

"I found it...! Help! Duverger! Du...."

... The dock was deserted. Water lapped against the piers of the bridge; the echo of the shadowy arch repeated the name in the silence... The river flowed lazily; gleams danced here and there, white and red... A slightly stronger wave lapped the shore near the rings... All was silent...

The Crows

When he'd finished his soup, Camus pushed away his plate. Elbows on the table, fists under his chin, he stared at the fireplace, following the gleams and shadows the flame spread over the ashes.

On the other side of the room, his wife came and went, fussing with plates, arranging silverware. A beam of light descended from the little lamp crowned with a green shade, floating between the floor and the ceiling striped with dark beams, illuminating only her skirt and hips. She closed the sideboard, pushed in the drawers and asked:

"You don't want anything else?"

"No," said Camus.

And he began to whistle a tune between his teeth. The woman pushed aside a curtain, pressed her forehead to the window, came back to the table and sat down:

"You're not saying anything…. What are you thinking about?"

He looked at her intensely and said slowly:

"What am I thinking…?"

Then his voice changed, and he finished in a detached tone:

"I'm thinking that it would be nice to stay here in the warmth, but that it's almost nine, and I must be leaving if I'm not to miss my train."

He pulled on a coat, pulled his cap on his head, picked up his stick in the corner and paused a moment on the doorstep.

"You won't be scared, all alone?"

She began to laugh. With a shrug of his shoulder he lifted on his coat, which had started to slip off.

"Then I'm going. Don't expect me before tomorrow night."

… The night was dark and quiet. The road, white with snow, blended with the fields.

Instead of going straight ahead, toward the village where lights shone in the depths of the valley, he turned onto a track. Now and then he looked back at his house, which seemed to sink away as he came down the hill. The front steps disappeared first, then the windows; the thatched roof touched the ground; the smoke that rose completely straight became less thick, was a cloud, then a shadow; and now he no longer made out anything but the countryside, white as far as the eye could see, piled up in places with mounds of snow, with some trees sagging under its weight, as if under heavy and delicious fruits.

Then he stopped to make sure of the path, feeling the ground with the tip of his stick, moving his feet forward carefully. Stones skittered away under his boots. He took a step back and listened. The small dry sound of pebbles shattering ice came to him, and he murmured: "I'm going the right way." Sitting on a bundle of sticks, coat rolled up on his knees, he reflected.

For three days, the same thought had taken such a strong hold of him that his brain opened at the exact place where he'd left it, just as a book on a bedside table opens to the same page read a hundred times.

His wife was cheating on him, the wife he'd married when she didn't have a sou; she was cheating on him with Pierre the cowherd! At first, he'd thought it was jealous slander, but after reading over and over the unsigned letter denouncing the culprits, he'd ended by doubting... then believing. Of course he'd been wrong to marry her, such a beautiful girl, so strong and young, when he was twenty-five years older. He hadn't made her unhappy, though. He'd satisfied her every whim, been attentive to her least desire. She was the richest and best dressed in the village, and as a reward for all that!... A thousand episodes jostled in his memory: bad moods for no reason, little things that were inexplicable at first, but became so clear once he knew!... Still, he hesitated, and wanting to have a clear heart, he'd pretended he'd take a trip, and left his home by this path. The lover would have to come this way, so as not to be met on the road.

He thought he heard the sound of footsteps muffled by snow in the distance. He crouched down. The noise came closer; a shadow fell across the path, growing larger, and when it was before him, he stood up abruptly.

"Stop there!"

The shadow didn't move. Camus made out a man, and when he recognized his features, he grabbed him by the collar, shouting in his face:

"Ah! This time around, I've got you, scoundrel!"

"You're mistaken," stammered the man, "You..."

Camus began to laugh, a terrible laugh:

"Ah! Ah! I've made a mistake then! Aren't you Pierre the cowherd, then...? Tell me what you're doing here, at this time.... No answer...? I'll tell you, I will: you're going to my wife, to my house!"

"Not at all...."

The old man gnashed his teeth:

"Shut up, liar! You're going there...! You wanted to see her? Well! I'll take you there! Let's go! Walk!"

He pushed him with all his strength, grunting as if

to spur on an unruly horse:

"Onward! Move! Gee-up!"

"But I tell you," repeated the other, half-strangled, "I'm not going there…"

"Onward!"

"But I repeat…"

Struggling, the man slipped and fell backward. Seized by a mad rage, seeing him on the ground, Camus began to cover his face with kicks and punches. The man got up again with a jerk, wiped the back of his hand on his face splattered with blood and cried:

"Alright! Yes! I'm going there, to your wife! Are you happy? And I'll keep coming, because she doesn't want any more of you, she doesn't want more…"

But as he was opening his mouth to spit more insults, the old man struck the stick on his head. He let out a great cry, took two steps back… collapsed… disappeared…

There was a half-second of dreadful silence, a few pebbles rolling and clattering… then a noise was heard, loud and deep…

Stick in hand, eyes dilated, Camus listened… Nothing stirred… There was nothing living around him… He stammered:

"I threw him in the gully!"

Suddenly, terror filling him, sweating with horror and fright, he began to run.

When he saw his home, a bit of calm returned to him, a sort of pride. He felt too old to have hit so hard. He was raising his fist to knock on the shutter when the door opened. On the threshold, he saw his wife, lamp in hand, leaning out. She said in a tender voice:

"Is that you, my darling?"

He was about to jump at her throat and scream with

wild joy:

"Your darling! Go reunite with him in his hole!"

But he pulled himself together:

"It's me, Camus!"

The circle of light that the lamp spread on the snow began to dance, and the woman stepped back. He came in. Without saying anything, he unbuttoned his coat, threw his cap on the table, took off his boots and sat down. He shivered near the burning fireplace and spoke low.

"I missed my train... The road is so bad..."

He stood up:

"Do you want to go to bed?"

There, he began to tremble. He felt his wife beside him, heard her breath, watched her movements and thought with a savage joy:

"She's not sleeping! She wonders why he hasn't come, if he saw me... if I have doubts... and she's afraid...! No one will ever know the truth. If someday the body is found, they'll say: The cowherd took the wrong path and plunged into the gully."

But little by little, terror invaded him:

"What if I didn't kill him, though? What if he's escaped, mutilated and bloody, and will accuse me, saying: It's Camus who pushed me?"

At that thought, a vision of policemen and judges passed before his eyes, and he buried his head in the pillow.

In the morning he got up, overcome by fatigue. The snow fell without stopping. All day long, he remained seated by the window, eyes lost between the heavy sky and white countryside, occasionally watching his wife come and go. Her cheeks were pale, her eyes sunken, and she shuddered at the crack of a branch, the loud and distant barking of a farm dog. She picked up her sewing without saying anything, then let the work drop on her lap... Night fell. Camus broke the silence.

"What are you thinking? You can't sew, it's too dark..."

She murmured: "That's true" and lit the lamp. He saw that large tears had left a trail glistening on her cheeks, and turned his head.

He didn't close his eyes at night. When the sun rose, he took up the same place by the window, gaze irresistibly drawn toward the same corner of horizon, guessing that under the thickest and whitest carpet was the gully into which the other had fallen.

This went on for five days. Then, one afternoon, the snow stopped falling and the sun turned the clouds yellow. He saw a swirling flock of crows, which made a black, moving spot on the bleak sky. From time to time one of the birds dropped down, then flew back up. Then another descended, then another...

At first, he followed their goings on mechanically. Then, their sudden cries piercing the silence, a thought came to him:

"But they're above the gully...! So...? They're coming there, drawn by something... by prey... by the body of the *other*...!"

He pushed back his chair with a gesture so violent his wife lifted her eyes toward him. Following his gaze, she also saw the black crows in the pale sky. He turned his head in her direction, eye lit by hate. A grimace tugged at his wrinkled face. He picked himself up from his chair, rubbed his hands together, lit his pipe, sat down and began to smoke, hands in his pockets, legs stretched out.

The woman remained motionless, watching the

birds. One of them lifted higher than the others, holding a rag in its beak. The old man began to snicker, as his wife, eyes wide open, clasped her hands and hid her face in her apron.

The day was ending. A shadow glided over the floor beams. Endless numbers of crows rose and fell in heavy flight, their cries gradually becoming less strident. Little by little, mysterious and calm, night closed in on the dreary sky.

Piquet?

When Ranaille heard himself condemned to the death penalty, he slumped forward with a sudden movement. Clenching his jaw, he looked for a long time at his enormous hands, useless now. His emotion lasted only a short time, however, and when a round of cheering started in the back of the room, he began to scream:

"You bunch of idlers! You slackers!"

He was full of such rage and furious energy that he had to be dragged from his seat, biting and half mad.

At night, he refused all food, and the guards heard him twisting in his straitjacket until morning, trying to break the ties. He fell asleep at last, overcome by fatigue, and the next morning his lawyer found him calm, mocking and boastful. As he'd become quiet again and seemed not even to remember his crisis, his shackles were removed that day. Free, he stretched out his powerful arms, passed a hand over his bull-like neck where the razor had just traced a cold path, shivered like a man waking up in a train at sunrise and said to his guard:

"A round of piquet…?"

Outside it was beautiful, and though the high walls of the prison tried to block them, rays of sunshine flowed through the bars, painting golden lines in the cell, along with red streaks that moved and changed, giving the gray walls and big table, with its dice cups, bottle of wine and cards the feel of a summer day in a tavern.

After he'd won, he leaned back a little on his stool and said, laughing:

"Well, old man? Another?"

"Another," agreed the guard.

Ranaille slowly shuffled the cards, and lifting his thumb to deal, asked:

"This won't last more than forty days, will it?"

Without waiting for an answer, he added:

"Well, I don't care. Here or at La Nouvelle, it's all the same..."

He didn't imagine for a moment that his charm might be rejected. For long months, with his muscles, fury and daring, he'd terrorized an entire neighborhood. Now he asked himself how anyone would dare stop him, and imagined they'd "look twice" before sending him to the scaffold. Sometimes, struck by doubt, he stared at his arms, clenched his fists, flexed his biceps so his shirt stretched tight and finally shrugged his shoulders, reassured by the show of his strength. He made plans, dreaming of a place in the tropics and catnaps in the shade of palm trees: a calm existence that was a little boring perhaps, but the reward for a successful escape. He forgot his arrest and conviction, and with no anxiety crossed the barrier of his third week, smoking, singing and sleeping well.

But in the middle of the twenty-second night, he had a nightmare and woke up drenched in sweat, deathly pale, calling: "Help!" — When asked what was wrong, he shook his head, replying: "Nothing.... Nothing...." in a choked voice, casting fierce looks at the wall, his guard and his own body. He wouldn't be able to sleep again knowing *that* night was coming, the night when eyes fixed on the door, he would await the gradual arrival of day for the last time.

Starting then, he became nervous and irritable. Something unmentionable rose up between his guards

135

and himself, something terrible. The thought of it could shut him up abruptly in the middle of a phrase, and leave him shivering for hours, his throat dry. He no longer sang, and overcome by sudden fits of anger, he threatened with furious cries to break everything, or kill someone. He raised his fists and yelled, "I am a man, you have no right!" That phrase "you have no right!" must have been the answer to some obstinate thought in his brain, for he kept repeating it, in reply to everything and nothing, with rage or sadness, breaking off a word or stopping a gesture to repeat in the same tone:

"You have no right. You have no right...!"

One day, since he was even more serious than usual, his guard suggested a game of piquet. He said "yes" without enthusiasm and played distractedly. Little by little, the game began to interest him. When it was over, he brought up a move, telling his partner why he'd played badly, and proposed:

"Another?"

He kept winning. He felt the beautiful carefreeness of the first days again. He laughed and whistled, all his thoughts concentrated on the twelve cards in his left hand, all the mystery of the future enclosed in the card he waved in the air with his right. A final thought, then a decided gesture: — "Let's go!" But the streak that had favored him at the start left him. He had bad games, and the cards came back poorly. He still whistled, but now it was with rage. When his guard counted sixty, Ranaille threw down his cards, losing his temper:

"What are you trying to prove with games like this?"

When he lost again, he said:

"I don't want to play anymore:

One day, seeing him in a mood like this, his guard

risked asking:

"So…? Still want to play a little round?"

He sat down, muttering, and lost again. Then, he flew into a terrible rage:

"That one doesn't count! It's not fair!"

He checked the math; his fury grew even more intense. He spat out his cigarette, a yellow color. His eyes were bloodshot, and the veins in his temples had swollen to the point of bursting. A straitjacket had to be put on him, just as on the first day, and just as on the first day he pulled at his ties like a trapped beast, until he turned to prayer and begged:

"They have no right… Take it off me…"

The next day, he asked shyly:

"Piquet?…"

In front of the cards, he got back a little of his cheerfulness. But he played badly, and when the game didn't give him a good result, he clenched his jaw and balled up his fists. Only the threat of the straitjacket calmed him, and as the game went on, he clawed the table and snarled insults with broken words. He'd begun to hate his guard, and watched his slightest gesture, eyes blazing like a tiger waiting for the right moment to leap on his prey.

To avoid a drama, the guard was replaced. He looked at the new man with suspicion at first. Although he had wanted to strangle the first, he was used to his ways, so abrupt and at times joking; he'd grown used to hating him, and now that was missing. Yet the new guard also proposed a round of piquet, which he accepted.

That was his thirtieth day in the cell, and the previous night he had begun to worry again, turning over in bed until morning. — But now he won. He played a second game, won again, and so on until night fell. Never in the last four weeks had the day seemed so light. He loved the game, less for the strategies than for the emotion of the win. Each game continued to be a success, and the idea of loss irritated and terrified him at the same time.

At night, he slept well. As soon as he got up, he would ask for the cards and begin to play and win.

The guard, as he'd been taught, set about losing. Appeased, Ranaille remained calm. The hours dragged on. After eight or so days, his streak unchallenged, Ranaille began to develop a suspicion. On various occasions the guard had omitted counting a fourteenth or fifteenth and played like a real apprentice, leaving him to take advantage at his leisure. He watched him, and was on the point of saying something, but in the end decided not to. He didn't think: "He lost on purpose," but "He's afraid to win," and feeling a bit of pride at causing this fear, he remained silent and satisfied. Fear was a tribute to the brute; it was respect.

So the afternoons continued to pass, but as the fortieth day approached, the convicted man once again began to suffer night terrors. The game wasn't enough to numb his mind. At the end of two or three rounds, he'd pushed away the cards, his gaze unfocused, his features drawn:

"I've had enough."

And he had to be begged:

"Come on... let's see... I'd like my revenge, just once..."

He picked up the game, still winning, but uninterested in it, now that he was sure to win. His thought would turn to something else, and he'd suddenly stare at his guard with silent anxiety, trying to glimpse his sentence in his eyes, tortured by a suspicion:

"Maybe he knows?…"

And at night, while trying to chase away the horrible vision in his head, which was like a relentless fly, the thought came to him: "My guard will know one day before me, all day… the last… and we'll be face to face, and he won't say to me: It's over… this is it… He'll keep the thought behind his forehead!…"

He had become polite, submissive and gentle with everyone, as if each person held part of the decisive power, as if each could appeal for presidential pardon. But he looked at those who approached with increasing anxiety, trying to find in their faces and attitudes a sign capable of giving him information, while fearing that sign with equal terror.

During the forty-third night he didn't sleep, listening to the noises from the street and chattering his teeth so loudly that he had to press his jaw into his chest so as not to bite. He didn't have the strength to sleep in that morning and pulled on his trousers, thinking he'd carry out the same gestures the next day. As soon as he was up, he sank his eyes into those of his guard, but saw nothing strange in the usual expression. He said to him, while dressing:

"It's too much, good God almighty! It's too much!"

The other replied:

"You look well today… Piquet?"

He said "No" and stayed in his cell until lunch. He ate little, stretched out on his bed, remained motionless.

At about three o'clock, he asked to play and handed a cigarette to his guard. The guard, eyes on the ground, refused.

He stopped shuffling his cards and stammered:

"What…"

He didn't finish the question and began to play with

clenched teeth, but paler now, with trembling hands. The guard no longer spoke either; nothing was heard but the thud of cards falling flat on the wood, and both remained with heads bent, stubbornly focusing on the game without looking at the other. They played quickly, nervously, no longer collecting their tricks.

"You must have finished?" Ranaille suddenly asked.

"No," replied the guard as if suddenly waking from a dream, "No..."

Ranaille counted:

"... I put down 2 and kept 3, and 2 five, and 4 nine, and 4 thirteen, and 5 eighteen, and 6 twenty-four... 242... You won. You..."

And suddenly, eyes open wide, he stammered:

"That's it... I'm done for... You know... They told you..."

"What?... But what?... Me?... No," said the guard, trembling.

Ranaille rolled over in his bed, and pressed his hands against his ears, sobbing:

"That's it, I tell you... That's it... You can see it on your face... And you forgot to lose..."

The guard half opened the door, and said in a low voice to his colleague in the hallway:

"You can come in now... he knows..."

Ranaille sobbed:

"That's it... you have no right... no right... no right..."

The guards were silent, unmoving. The sound of hooves came up to them from the stable yard. In the street the muffled murmurs of night could be heard... The sun sank gently in the calm sky, leaving a little red on the horizon.

On the Road

The tramp sat by the roadside.

For two days he'd walked under the heavy sun, going wherever his feet carried him. At night he rested under a haystack, and continued on his wandering way at
dawn. As soon as he arrived at the doorstep of a house,
with his wild look, unkempt beard and rags, the women
clutched their little ones to their skirts. In the fields, as
soon as he asked for work, ready to take on any tasks,
they pushed him away roughly. Head slightly lowered
and stick trailing after him, he set off again, resigned.
But after a few steps, when he was sure they could not
see him, he wiped away the big tears streaming down his
cheeks with the back of his hand.

Now, however, he began to feel rebellious, a rebellion that came from his hungry belly, and despite himself
the words escaped from his lips:

"It's not fair!... There is no God!"

He raised his stick as he cursed, but when it hit the
earth, he saw something bright jump up, then fall with a
clear sound.

Stooping over, he looked in the dust:

"Now that's luck!..."

He turned over again and again between his fingers
the piece of gold he'd just picked up. He blew on it, not
daring to believe such a windfall.

"A louis!... a real one!... I haven't had one for such
a long time! I'm going to eat my fill, drink all I like and
sleep in a bed... With this, and working on the way, I

can make it to town… There, I always find something."

He thought: But the money isn't mine!… What if someone saw me?… He looked around. No one. He was alone, all alone on the road.

Far away, to the right, above the golden wheat, a village seemed to arch up on the horizon. He could just make out the thatched roofs and the pointed bell tower. Making his way across the fields gaily, singing on his way, long ears of wheat brushing against him, he started off.

In front of an inn, he stopped:

"Hello, everyone!…"

A woman blocked the door, and asked:

"What do you want?"

"I'd like to eat."

"We haven't got any leftovers… Move along…"

He blinked:

"Oh!… I'm not asking for charity! I'll pay!"

He flipped the louis over in his hand.

Astonished to see gold between the fingers of a vagabond, the peasant called her husband. He looked suspiciously at the man and the twenty francs, then asked:

"Where did you get that?"

"What's it to you, if I pay?"

"Well! I don't want to sell you anything to eat!…"

The tramp was silent for a few seconds. Then he put the piece of gold back in his pocket, shrugged and went on his way.

The innkeeper and his wife followed him with their eyes.

"He must have gotten his hands dirty somehow to get a hold of that."

"Should we warn the police?"

A customer arrived. He was told the adventure, already exaggerated:

"A pauper, with a look that would terrify you, wanted to pay me a louis. — That's not normal. — There were others clinking in his pockets. These scoundrels, you never know where they come from, where they're going…"

In five minutes he was reported in the village. Kids followed him from afar, hostile, and he, dragging his tired feet, looked with astonishment and incomprehension at the faces staring at him.

Any other day, he'd have taken offense, but as he had money it hardly worried him.

The baker in his shop was setting out loaves of bread, the big brown kind, with a good crisp crust.

"Hello, sir. I'd like one round loaf."

"Off you go."

"Oh! You're so untrusting in this part of the country! Just because someone doesn't have fine clothes, doesn't mean he'll stretch out his hand. You'll be paid."

He held out his louis.

"I told you to get on your way!"

He remained standing with his arm held out, speechless.

"Ah! You don't want it?… You…"

He nodded, whispered: "Fool!…" and left.

Everywhere, at the grocer, at the cheese shop, at the butcher, came the same response.

He wondered: Why don't they want to sell to me, if I can pay? Maybe my coin is worthless?…

He didn't dare go out. He felt the metal deep in his pocket, so small and hot from his touch, shiny and soft amidst the lumps of hardened bread and crumbs of tobacco.

Evening came. He still hadn't eaten. He'd taken the main road again, and while walking, reflected:

"But I'm not going to starve with twenty francs on me!"

Little by little, however, he began to understand.

"No, I don't look like someone who has a louis. Gold, in the hands of a worthless wretch like me, seems suspicious. They wonder where I got it... maybe they think I stole it... that I attacked a passerby in a corner of the woods. Hunger can give you such a strange face!..."

While he was speaking to himself like this, at a bend in the road, he saw someone coming toward him. It was a man, and he also walked with a shuffling step and curved back. His clothes were worn out, and an old hat covered his head. His unkempt beard, gray with dust, only better emphasized the bronze color of his face.

As if all those who have suffered know one another, the two vagabonds stopped and shook hands.

"Where are you going, friend?" asked the man with the louis.

"I'm trying to make it to the village over there, to spend the night. Shall we walk together?"

"No, I'm going the opposite way. And if I have advice to give you, it's to turn back... They're hardly welcoming to tramps over there... I've just come from that direction. You won't find a corner of a barn to sleep in."

"What! Even with money..."

"Even with money."

He was going to say "especially", but remained silent. The other went on:

"The peasants are the same everywhere. As long as they think they're being asked for charity, they turn a deaf ear. But when they're shown this..."

He shook a few sous in his hand, and began to

laugh:

"It's not much! Seventeen sous! But it'll be enough for three days."

As soon as he spoke, the one who hadn't eaten thought:

"With seventeen sous, he's richer than I am with twenty francs! He'll find bread, a bale of straw to rest his head..."

An idea came to him:

"Listen, give me something...

The other immediately closed his hands on the sous:

"I can't, friend! I have just enough to reach the village... and no more!..."

"You don't have any bread?"

The other shook his bag and said:

"No... Goodbye."

He took a step. The tramp stopped him.

"You're not going to leave like that and let me die on this spot..."

"I have nothing."

"But you do, you have those sous!... Let's see them... We're brothers on the road..."

"I can't... I just explained... On the way, you'll find work..."

The hunger, the horrible hunger gnawing at the belly of the vagabond, made him feel strangely intoxicated.

"Listen, I'll buy them from you, your sous. Yes, and I'll pay you well... I'll give you twenty francs..."

The other opened his eyes wide.

He went on, very quickly:

"Yes, twenty francs. I found them this morning, in the dust. But they refuse me everywhere, because I'm too ragged. Look, it's not clothes I have... It's rags. And hunger makes the eyes shine, gives you a mean-looking face... people are afraid. You have cleaner clothes, and with your big coat you look like a shepherd on a journey... Twenty francs in your hands won't be surprising. Anyway, you haven't suffered as much as I have... you've eaten this afternoon... I haven't for two days... I'm hungry..."

He said these last words in a low voice, ashamed, but he looked terrifying as he leaned his face into the other's.

"The market is good... Are you afraid it's false? Hey... Listen to the sound ... There it is... Give me your sous..."

But the man moved away, pushing away the coin held out.

"Keep your money! You're richer than I am!"

"You don't understand, I can't use it... They don't want it... Give me your sous..."

"No... No... Goodbye!..."

Madness seized the mind of the tramp. In a rage, he clenched his jaw, closed his fists and violently grabbed the other by the throat:

"Give them to me..."

The man struggled, trying to escape the grip. He held out his arms and slipped, his fingers hooked. His mouth widened trying to cry out; his eyes opened and rolled upward in a frenzy... He fell... The sous rolled on the ground.

Groping on all fours, the murderer picked them up without counting, and began to run.

When the first lights of the village appeared, he stopped, panting. He realized then that he had the louis between his teeth. He felt the little coins in his pocket. He realized the horror of his crime... He was afraid... But hunger twisted his insides. He took the piece of gold and threw it, so it went flying.

In the leaves, there was a small shiver, like a fallen branch sliding into foam...

With long strides, he made it to the village:

"Four sous of bread, please?"

The baker took a loaf and handed it to him. The feel of the sous all covered in dust made him tremble.

But the bread was white and the crust golden. He bit into it eagerly, staggered out and plunged into the quiet night, only disturbed from time to time by the fall of a branch on dry leaves... The same sound that just now, his coin had made while falling.

The Culprit

"Your name, age, profession?"

In the courtroom, under the harsh light falling from the high windows, a little old man with a gentle face framed in white sideburns stood up.

Facing the president, he replied in a voice that trembled slightly:

"Maindrot, Jacques, eighty years old, independent income."

"That's alright, you may sit down."

Once the accusation had been read, the president spoke again: "You heard. You are charged with killing your wife, who was seventy-five years old, on the night of 17 to 18 November. Until then you had been a good man. You have never been convicted. Do you have something to say in your defense?"

"Mr. President, I'll give an explanation, if you allow me."

"Address yourself to the gentlemen of the jury."

Then, after acknowledging them with a short bow, the little old man began to speak slowly, searching for words, as if he were worried about the correctness of his language. He spoke in a distant voice, politely and softly, hat in hand, and despite themselves, the court and jury were moved by the majesty of his age. They listened without interruption to this elderly man, who had come before them with carefully chosen words, to defend his head.

"To explain, if not justify myself in your eyes, I

must go very far back in my memories. When I was twenty-five years old, left without parents, alone in the world, possessed of a small sum that enabled me to live without worrying about the next day, I made a marriage of love. Those words do not sound proper in the mouth of an old man, but it is necessary that you know.

For ten years I was the happiest man in the world. I loved my wife, and she loved me. There was a cloud: We didn't have a child, but we loved each other so much that I don't know what place we could have made in our affection for a little being had it come. At last we no longer thought of it, and did not regret anything.

Our life flowed on that way, gently and lightly, without conflict and without suspicion.

Now, gentlemen of the jury, I must tell you that at my age we defend our future less than our past, and so I speak to you with all the frankness and truth in my soul, as if to those confessors who will likely be my last."

He paused, and with trembling hands took his handkerchief and wiped his forehead.

He went on:

"Did I have to pay dearly for all my happiness? One day a suspicion crept into my mind. One of my friends, the oldest and best, began to show my wife a disturbing attention, flatteries she never rejected. How did I notice?... His gestures, his words, his 'nothing', all those tiny things are still enough to sink my heart and trouble my reason. From then on, I knew doubt. I spent hours at night searching for the fleeting glow that would guide my steps. I spied on them, I followed them, but I found nothing. I became hateful and mean, but how could I make a scene based only on a suspicion, without proof? I swear to you that if I'd surprised them in each others' arms, I could have killed them both in a fit of rage. I wouldn't have been surprised for a second, so sure was I and so keenly did I feel my betrayal.

That life lasted for years. For years I searched without finding a thing. And then I began to feel guilt, and spread over my memories a layer of 'forgive and forget'. I ended up believing that I had been wrong, and the calm returned to me that I'd felt in the past, without either my friend or my wife suspecting anything.

When my friend died a few years ago, I cried for him as one does for a brother, and the tears my wife poured on him did not surprise me. We were already old: she was sixty-five, I was seventy.

The years went on. Then one day, pushed by I don't know what vision of the future, the thought came to me of our approaching end. I told myself that at my age every hour is hard earned, and that it's good at the decline of life, when the day is ending, to know where you'll rest your head for eternity. I had already lived enough, and been happy, and I thought with great sweetness of the grave sheltered by trees, the flowers that would adorn the marble slab...

I spoke of this to my wife, and she smiled:

'I thought of all this well before you,' she said, 'and at the back of the cemetery in Montmartre, in a very calm and remote corner, I've chosen the place where we'll sleep side by side.'

She told me where it was, and I went to visit.

While walking amongst the tombs, I thought: 'Love gives two beings such similar thoughts, and we are still so close to one another. So why shouldn't similar dreams come to cradle us both?'

At the end of a walkway, I stopped. There it was: a piece of land with wild grass, completely surrounded by graves.

Out of curiosity, as one looks into the carriage of people traveling beside you, I glanced at the neighboring graves. And there, on the nearest one, I read the name of my friend.

Then I recognized the path I had traveled, and saw the dried flowers and wreaths we put there every year.

This realization stung me like the blow of a whip; it dazzled me like the glow of fire. All of a sudden, my whole past, all my suspicions and hates, rose up before me.

Our place? Near him? And she was the one who'd chosen it?

When I arrived back home, I must have looked like a madman. At dinner, I didn't eat a thing.

It was 17 November.

'What's wrong, love?' my wife asked.

'With me?... Nothing.'

'But yes, there's something...'

It might have been ten. In the street, all the sounds were muffled in the sadness of that autumn night.

'Well, you're right. I have something to say, and I'll tell you what it is. You were the mistress of Fromont, and for twenty years you have deceived me, you wretch!'

She went pale. Terror passed over her poor, old little face.

I no longer know if it was surprise or terror.

'For twenty years, do you hear me, our whole youth, my whole life... Ah! Don't I see clearly now? Don't I understand everything? How my suspicions were justified? How I regretting having dared brush you with a shadow of doubt? How you were sure you'd gotten away with it, and wanted to chase after him even in death? How you desired to lie between your husband

and lover? Is that how you envisioned us... underground?'

Madness took hold me. I walked toward her and took her neck in my hands. I must have clenched it tightly; I don't remember anything else. I don't know what anguish made her eyes roll upward. Then the light went out. In the street a dog began to howl at the moon. They found me there in the morning... That's all..."

He sat down. Big tears ran down his ivory-colored cheeks.

Briefly the lawyer stated the defense. The prosecutor replied with a few words, and the jury returned a verdict of "not guilty".

The Beggar

As evening began to fall, the beggar chose a spot in a ditch on the roadside, wrapped himself in the bag that served as his coat, put the thin package he was carrying at the end of a stick under his head, and almost fainting from fatigue and hunger, looked up at the dark sky filled with stars.

The road that stretched between the thick woods was deserted. In the trees, the birds were sleeping. The village in the distance was a big black shadow. All alone, in the calm and silence, the old man began to cry.

He had never known his parents. Raised by charity on a farm when he was small, now he roamed the highways, in search of a bit of work and some bread. Life had been hard to him. He had known all the griefs: the long winter nights at the foot of a haystack, the shame of begging, the desire to die, to fall asleep once and for all. He had never met anyone except suspicious and wicked men. What most filled him with sorrow was that the innocent seemed to fear him: children fled when they saw him, and dogs barked at his dusty rags.

Yet he was without bitterness or hate; he was only sad and very gentle.

He was dozing off, when in the distance, he heard some bells jingle. He looked up and saw a glimmer dancing above the ground, at the end of the road. A big horse pulled along a heavy cart, lifted so high up and stretching so wide that it seemed to fill the whole road. A man was walking next to the horse, and singing a song.

Then there was a brief silence when the cart hit a slope in the road. The hooves of the horse started to scrape and rasp more roughly against the stones. The man spurred on the animal with his voice and whip:

"Gee-up!... Gee!"

The animal pulled with its full chest, its neck outstretched. Two or three times, it slipped, fell almost to its knees, got up and made another effort, one which rippled its whole coat from shoulder to haunch. But it was out of breath, and the carriage stopped.

The driver, shoulder to the wheel, hands on the spokes, shouted more loudly:

"Gee! Gee... up!..."

The horse pulled with all its muscles, but the carriage did not move.

"Gee up! Gee!..."

The animal, legs spread, nostrils flared, no longer moved, trembling, clinging to the ground with its four iron-covered hooves so that it wouldn't be pulled backward by the enormous weight.

The driver, still braced, saw the beggar sitting on the edge of the ditch, and called out:

"A hand, comrade! This one doesn't want to move anymore. Come help give the cart a push."

The beggar got up and added his meager effort to the man's.

Both shouted:

"Gee, gee!..."

It was useless.

Exhausted and miserable, the poor man said:

"Let it catch its breath. The load is too heavy."

"Of course not. This one's a lazybones! If we take off the cart, we'll never be able to get it back on once we're over the hill. Hey! Ho!... Pass me a stone to wedge under the wheel. Let's do it by pushing it over to get started..."

The beggar picked up a stone and held it out.

"Look," said the driver. "I'll stay at the wheel. There's the whip. Take the horse by the ears, and set it going with big blows on the legs, leaning left. It'll take off."

Stung with pain, the horse made an effort. The earth wore down under its hooves, pebbles skittered away.

"It's going! It's going!"

As the horse threw itself forward, the driver leaned over to place the stone under the wheel, and took a misstep. The horse gave a slight kick, and the man let out a scream and fell.

He lay on his back, face convulsed, eyes haggard, elbows glued to the ground, strong hands gripping the circle of the wheel, trying to stop it from piercing his chest.

In a panicked voice, he shouted to the beggar:

"Forward! Forward! It's crushing me!..."

The other, guessing without seeing what had happened, began to strike the horse at random with his whip and a stick. But the exhausted horse dropped to its knees and rolled over on its side, and the cart fell forward. Its two front axles hit the ground, and the lantern hanging under its bottom went out. Nothing more was heard in the dark night but the quick breathing of the horse, and the suffocated rattle of the man moaning:

"Forward!... Forward!..."

Incapable of lifting the animal, the beggar ran to the driver and tried to pull him out. But he was caught tight under the wheel. With great effort, he was holding it a few centimeters from his torso: one false move, one

lapse, and he would be crushed to death... He understood this so well that when he saw the beggar lean over
he yelled:

"Don't touch! Don't touch!... Run to the village...
Quick... To my parents' house... The name is Luchat...
Last farm on the right... Tell them... Come with every-
one's help... I have another ten minutes... Go quick..."

The beggar raced up the hill as fast as he could. He
entered the village, running straight ahead. All the shutters were closed, and not a light was on. Behind the
gates the stable yards were deserted. A smell emerged,
sharp, pungent and warm, the smell of manure from the
stable and sour dairy milk. Dogs barked as he passed.
But he heard nothing, looked at nothing, his mind full of
the terrifying vision of the man knocked to the ground,
holding up with his fists the cart ready to crush him.

At last he stopped. Before him lay the path, all flat.
On his right was a building on the side of the yard. A
little light slipped through the slats of the blinds. He said
to himself: "There it is!" And with his fist, he hit the
shutters.

A voice asked:

"Is that you, Jules?"

Breathless from the speed of his run, he could not
answer, and knocked again. He heard the sound of a bed
creaking, steps on the floor. The window opened, and in
a square of light, the head of a man appeared, sleepy.

"Is that you, Jules?"

He had regained his breath a bit, and said, his words
short:

"No, but I've come to..."

The farmer didn't let him finish:

"Well, that's the way! Waking everyone up at this
time!"

He slammed the window shut and growled into the room.

"A waster!... A guttersnipe!..."

The beggar stood motionless and dazed, without a word, so brutal had the response been. He thought:

"What did he think I wanted? I didn't do anything bad, but... No doubt, I surprised him in his sleep... If he only knew, the good man!..."

Once again, timidly, he began to knock on the shutter.

From inside, the voice shouted:

"That's done now, eh?... You just see if I get up!"

Courage and breath returned to him, and he cried:

"Open!..."

"You go on your way..."

"Open!..."

This time the window opened, and with such force he had to jump aside so as not to be slapped by the shutters. The farmer had a mean look on his face, and a shotgun in his hand.

"Listen up, starving man, if you don't get moving, and quick, I'll give you a piece of this!"

From the bed, a shrill female voice shouted:

"Shoot him... It'll be a service to everyone. All they're good for is stirring up trouble, these prowlers... for stealing... or worse!"

Facing the pointed shotgun, the beggar was afraid, and sank back into shadow. He shuddered, almost forgetting the poor soul who was dying at that moment on the road. For the first time, resentment filled his heart. Never had he felt so pathetic and rejected.

And what if he had been hungry, what if he'd knocked to ask for shelter? Didn't he have the right, miserable as he was, to find a heap of straw near the animals, a bit of bread for the dogs?... Wasn't he, in his rags, a creature of the good God just like others, even if the rich threatened him with death?...

Fear, in a single moment, had made him angry.

First he wanted to rush with blows of his stick against the shutters, then he reflected:

"If I knock now, he'll shoot... If I call out, he'll rouse the village and I'll be knocked out before I can say where I've come from... If I go somewhere else, it'll be the same..."

His resolution made, he began to run, retracing the path traveled, to try and save his momentary companion all by himself. He ran, terrified of what might have happened during his absence...

"What am I going to find down there!..."

Hurtling down the hill, he felt he had the legs of a twenty year old again. When he approached the place where the cart had stopped, he cried:

"Comrade!"

No answer. He shouted again:

"Comrade!"

The darkness was so deep he couldn't even make out the horse and cart. Suddenly, he heard a whinny. He moved forward. A few feet away, the horse was still lying on its side, with the cart plunged forward.

"Comrade! Comrade!"

He bent down, and when the moon came out from behind a cloud, he could see the man lying down, arms outstretched, eyes closed, mouth bleeding, under the enormous wheel buried in his chest!

Unable to help that poor mutilated being, he felt a furious rage for the parents. Filled with a terrible need for revenge, he galloped in a straight dash down to the farm, and this time, without worrying about the threat of the shotgun, overcome entirely by the thought of the wild joy he would experience, fists clenched tight, he pounded on the shutters.

"Is that you, Jules?"

He didn't answer. When the window opened, he saw the wicked face of the father and heard him ask again:

"Is that you, Jules?"

He shouted:

"No! It's the starving man from before who'd come to tell you your boy was dying on the road."

Two terrified voices — that of the father and the mother — spoke at once:

"What did you say... What did you say?... Come in quick..."

But he, pulling his hat over his eyes and moving away with quick steps, said:

"Excuse me... I'm in a rush now... But there's no need for you to hurry. It's too late... When I came the first time, then it was necessary to hurry, for he was going to be crushed. By now, he already has the whole load of hay on his ribs!"

The woman sobbed:

"Go, my husband... Run..."

And the husband shouted, groping for his clothes:

"Where is he?... Listen here... For the love of God..."

The beggar, stick on his shoulder, plunged into the night, until he could no longer hear the weeping of the two old people.

In the courtyard, a rooster woke everyone early with its noise, and the dog with its nose at the gate howled for a long time at the moon.

Confrontation

Facing death, the man did not flinch.

Eyes half-closed, he looked at the marble slab where there rested milky-white flesh, the reddish gash of a knife wound between the breasts. The rigid body had kept its shape and seemed living. Only the hands, with their violet nails and overly translucent skin, the wide-open, murky and listless eyes, and the darkened mouth laughing a horrible laugh, gave the feeling of eternal sleep.

In the room with the cold walls and gray tiles, an oppressive silence weighed. On the ground, near the dead woman, the sheet that had been thrown off earlier still bore traces of blood. The judges observed the accused, who stood up straight, between two guards, maintaining an aloof attitude. He held his hands behind his back, his chest inflated, his face impassive.

The examining magistrate spoke:

"Well, Gautet, do you recognize your victim?"

The man turned his head, looked at everything around the judge and corpse as if trying to recall some very distant memory, and replied slowly:

"I do not know this woman, Judge. I've never seen her before."

"But the witnesses claim you did, and they are positive you were her lover…"

"The witnesses are mistaken, sir. I do not know this woman."

"Come now," said the judge after a moment of silence, "What good is it trying to deceive us? This confrontation is a simple formality, unnecessary in your case. You're intelligent. It would be in your interest, if you want to acquire any right to the jury's leniency, to confess!..."

"I cannot confess, being innocent."

"Once again, remember that your denials have no significance. For my part, I am inclined to believe that you gave in during a moment of passion, one of those moments of madness that make one see red... But look at you now, in front of your victim... You don't seem to repent one bit, or show any emotion..."

"Repent?... Of course not. I cannot repent, not being a criminal... As for my emotion, my God, if it has not been destroyed, it has been greatly reduced, for the simple reason that I knew when I entered this place what you were going to make me see. I'm no more moved than you are. I don't make a crime of your coldness: what right do you have to reproach me for mine?"

He spoke in a flat voice, without a gesture, a perfect master of himself, without seeming worried about the overwhelming charges piled up against him. He confined all his explanations to a cold, stubborn denial.

One of the assistants said softly:

"He won't give away anything... He'll deny it even on the scaffold."

And the judge replied without anger:

"Precisely, sir, on the scaffold."

This pitched battle between prosecutor and accused, this persistent "no" opposing all questions against what appeared to be the evidence of facts, had something irritating about it that exaggerated the stormy atmosphere outside even more. Beyond the frosted windows, the sun was going down, illuminating the corpse with a uniform yellow glow.

"So," said the examining magistrate again: "You do not recognize the victim. What about this?"

He lay before the defendant a large ivory-handled knife, with a heavy blade spattered in blood.

The man picked up the weapon, looked at it a few moments, then handed it to one of the guards and wiped his fingers.

"This?… I've never seen it either."

"It's clear," the judge sneered. "This knife is yours. It was hanging in your study. Twenty people saw it in your apartment."

The accused nodded.

"That simply proves twenty people are mistaken."

"Let's end with this," said the judge. "Although your guilt may be beyond the shadow of a doubt, we will attempt a decisive demonstration. The victim shows the marks of strangulation on her neck. One can see the clear trace of five fingers, particularly long ones, according to the coroner. Show your hands to these men. Good."

The judge lifted the chin of the dead woman.

On her neck, there were violet lines that contrasted with her white skin; at the end of each bruise, the flesh was cut open deeply, as if a nail had been pressed into it. The marks looked like the dark veins of a giant leaf.

"Look at your work. As you were trying to strangle this unfortunate woman with your left hand, with your free right hand you thrust that knife into her chest. Come here, and do just as you did the night of the murder. Put your fingers on the bruises that I just showed you… Come on…"

Gautet hesitated, then shrugged and said in a lower voice:

"You want to see if my fingers match?… And

then?… What will that prove?"

He stepped forward toward the slab, a little paler, jaw clenched and eyes dilated. For a moment he stood motionless, his eyes fixed on the stiffened corpse, then with an automatic gesture he reached out his hand and laid it on the flesh.

The clammy cold of contact made him shudder imperceptibly, and his fingers suddenly contorted, as if to strangle.

Under the grasp, the frozen muscles of the dead woman seemed to waken. They could be seen stretching obliquely, from the clavicles to the angles of the jaw. The mouth abandoned its rictus of horror and opened in a dreadful yawn, so that the dried lips opened, showing teeth encrusted in a brown coating.

A chill passed through the audience.

That gaping mouth in the woman's impassive face, that mouth that opened like a groan from beyond the grave, with its dry, coarse, blue tongue twisted over itself in the depths, had something enigmatic and terrifying about it.

And suddenly, from this black hole, there came a confused murmur, a kind of buzzing. Then a huge fly with a blue belly and shimmering wings, one of those filthy vulture flies that lives off death, began to whirl and whistle around its cave, as if defending the entrance, before suddenly coming to rest on Gautet's white lips.

With a gesture of disgust, he tried to shoo it away; but the beast came back, clinging to his flesh with all the strength of its poisoned legs.

With a bound, the man recoiled backward, his eyes wild, his hair standing on end, his hands outstretched, his whole body shivering, and he began to scream with a crazed voice:

"I confess!... It was me!... Take me away!... Take her away!..."

The Empty House

Once the lock had been picked, the man entered, closed the door carefully and stopped to listen.

He knew the empty house well, but the deep silence that night impressed him. Never had he experienced such desire and fear of loneliness. He held out his hand, brushed the wall and slid the bolt. Only now, somewhat reassured, did he pull from his pocket a small electric lamp and look around. The light projected pale beams into the shadows that danced with each beat of his heart. To give himself courage, he murmured:

"I'm home!"

He began to laugh, then went into the dining room.

Everything was in meticulous order. Four chairs were arranged around the table; the spindly legs of another, near the window were mirrored on the shiny floor. A light scent of fruits and tobacco floated through the air. He opened the drawers of the sideboard where silver cutlery was neatly kept, thinking: "It's better than nothing," before putting it in his pocket. But with each step, the cutlery clinked and clanged against him, and fearing the noise he made, which might wake someone, he tiptoed away, neglecting the silver-gilt spoons and small pearl-handled knives glimpsed at the back of the case. To excuse his weakness, he told himself:

"They're not what I came for…"

Arriving at the table, however, he stopped undecided, feeling the forks weighing in the depth of his pocket. He was hesitant to enter the little living room where the shadow — thanks to the drawn curtains, no doubt — seemed more mysterious. Ashamed of feeling so cowardly, he took one step, then another, bold and composed, like a peaceful bourgeois who returns home at night, his daily shift completed. He was no longer cold, no longer afraid, and noticing a torch topped with candles on a piece of furniture, he took it, lit it and raised it a little, examining the photographs hanging in gold frames on the wall, knick-knacks, piano and fireplace smelling of cold ashes and soot. He took a good look around the room, lifted up some papers with a finger, sized up the worth of a statuette, put it back and pulled out a small lamp, before pushing open the door of the bedroom.

There, he hesitated yet again. As he had come a few days earlier on the pretext of visiting the apartment, he remembered the place of each piece of furniture, the shape of every last object. One look had been enough to see the stocky dresser where the old man shut away his valuables, the cabinet where he put his money, the bed half-hidden by the alcove and the mirrored wardrobe where he might later make a rapid and fruitful inventory. Then he put out the lamp, and without knocking into any chair, arms stretched out, he walked straight to the dresser. He felt the marble, slid his hand along its sides like a horse-trader who pats the belly of a filly, and like a good worker, one finger of his left hand resting on the lock, searched in his pocket for his bunch of keys.

He was a little less calm than he had been earlier. What made him nervous now wasn't the anxiety of being alone at night or robbing another's house, but the feverish haste of a player holding a card, gripping it and weighing it before turning it over. What would he find in a moment?... Securities?... Bank notes?... How many?

What fortune rested there, defended by a single board?...

He was still looking for his keys without managing to find them. Earlier, putting the silverware in his pocket, he hadn't thought to pull out his tools and everything had gotten tangled up.

Spoons passed through the rings of picklocks, forks crossed their tines and twisted with his efforts, tearing the lining of his pocket, clawing his skin. Hurrying to finish, he stamped his foot, swore, clenched his jaw and pulled so violently that the fabric gave way, while the false keys and cutlery fell in a jumble on the floor with a great metallic clanking... He was still nervous... The goal was so close, but time was passing!... He no longer knew the hour, precisely; it only seemed to him that long minutes had flowed by since he entered. The clock on the wall, whose tick-tock he had not noticed until then, beat at short rapid intervals...

Kneeling in front of the dresser, he took one of the hooks and tried it, ear pressed to the lock: the bolt resisted. It took another, a new one, and yet another, turning in small cautious strokes... Nothing! Still nothing!... Overcome once again by anger, he burst into laughter:

"No!... I won't spare the furniture!"

And grabbing a chisel coldly, with a single thought he broke the lock. Then he opened the drawer and lit the lamp.

In front of the banknotes gathered into bundles, he gave a sigh of joy. Slowly, calmly, he took them, counted them, looked at them openly, and stroked them with the back of his hand. So as to be more at ease, he sat down as he continued his search. Beneath a golden scroll, there was a thick packet of registered securities, for nearly twenty thousand francs — a fortune!... He thought:

"What a shame to leave that!... Well!..."

He put them back. He lingered over the loot, weighing the gold coins, reading their dates, comparing the surfaces and feel the of fifty and forty franc pieces before making them disappear into the pocket of his jacket. He no longer felt haste or anger, simply a great well-being, peace, success at having driven away terror. A heavy car crossed the street, shaking the windows, making the furniture tremble and the coins scattered on the floor vibrate imperceptibly. This simple noise brought him back to reality. He looked at his watch: four o'clock — and thought: "Already?..." — Picking up the coins without counting them, he searched the other drawers. But he found nothing interesting. Amongst the papers and letters, a little money had been forgotten. He put it in his waistcoat pocket, a mechanical gesture, got up again, knees numb, and murmured:

"How convenient."

Before him, on a table, he saw a bronze paper-weight. He had been wise enough to neglect the jewelry and registered securities which were too compromising, offering himself, in addition to what was useful, this pleasant little souvenir... He put out his hand. But at the same moment the clock, whose rushed tick-tock was hurrying toward the hour, struck a sharp note... He remained with his hand outstretched, his fingers open...

The silence, struck through for an instant by this weak sound, suddenly seemed heavy and solemn. Nothing else vibrated between those four walls, not even the imperceptible murmur of the fabrics where the folds were bunched together, or the creaking of dry wood that lies dormant during the day and dies slowly night after night... His ears were filled with the humming of the blood that moved through his head, beating at his temples, constricting his vessels... Fear had taken hold of him, idiotic and unexpected, the fear of no longer hearing anything: where did that strange silence come from in which nothing dared move?...

He had put out the lamp, and in the darkness, shoulders hunched forward, craning his neck, nostrils flared, ears open, he leaned toward the fireplace, where earlier the little clock had beat so fast... The tick-tock had gone silent! The clock had stopped. What could have been more simple?... Yet a shiver ran down the length of his neck; he had the feeling of a secret and immediate danger. Grabbing his knife, he lit the lamp and turned into a bedroom.

In the alcove, half-emerging from the shadows, a face with an open mouth and terrible eyes looked at him. He felt that his presence did not frighten the face, that its eyes did not flee his, that its long hand clinging to the sheet did not tremble, that the skinny leg sticking out of the blankets would straighten out, that someone would at last stand before him and take him by the throat, that he would feel the breath of the pale impassive old man on his face.

Without daring move his head, he looked for the door with his eyes. He no longer thought of the bank notes on the ground: he thought only of fleeing. But with those eyes on him, he understood he would never reach the door. He imagined the old man would open his mouth to cry: "Help!" and that once this was done he'd no longer have time to escape. And so, without reflecting further, with a leap like a beast attacking, he rushed toward the bed, lifted his knife, and with gasps of rage, twice plunged it in to the hilt. Not a cry, not a groan was heard; only the soft echoless fall of a pillow disturbed the silence. Then the head fell back, lips parted.

Still trembling with fear and rage, he took a step back and contemplated his work. His lamp gave off such a weak light that in the disorder of the crumpled shirt, he could not make out even the trace of his blade, or the blood from the wounds. He must have hit soundly and on target, for the face of the old man had not even changed. With the first blow, quick and magnificent, he had been stopped clean in his tracks, as if by a bullet. Pride filled him at his mastery, and he growled, threatening:

"Ah! You were there?... Well, now you see, eh?..."

Yet leaning over the motionless face, the thought suddenly came to him, as the features had changed so little, that though he had struck through the bedcovers, perhaps the old man was not dead, and that he was still looking at him with supreme irony.

For the second time, he raised his knife and struck, lifted it and struck again with a wild frenzy, intoxicated by the dull sound of the tip piercing the chest, growing excited as he plunged the blade in with curses and cries, indifferent to the danger of waking the house. The shirt was no more than rags now, and the skin an open wound. Only the face, which no stab had pierced, kept its impressive calm. Half-mad, the man grabbed his lamp and took his victim by the throat to strike one last time.

But his raised right fist remained in the air and a cry died on his lips: For under his hand, he came to feel, not the moist and twitching flesh from which life has just escaped with rivers of blood, but a flesh that no tremor could make shudder, cold with that terrible cold like nothing else; dead flesh, dead for many hours!... And his arm fell...

Crime had never frightened him. He had seen his

knife red often, and felt the hot spurt of severed arteries in his face; he knew the smell of blood, the rattle of the body expiring... To cause death was nothing... But this!... A sudden respect woke in his murderous soul, leaving him motionless, a superstitious terror of the great mystery that froze him... He had believed the house empty, and had entered the house of a dead man!... He had almost stolen from a dead man!... A dead man!... So that is where the frightening silence and overly darkness had come from!...

Far, far away a clock struck five. Without daring turn his head toward the forgotten loot, cap in his hands, eyes dilated, with a great fear filled by memories of prayers, he backed out of the room, stumbled against the furniture and ran off into the night, away from this death for which he had not been responsible...

A Maniac

He was neither wicked nor bloodthirsty. He simply had a very special understanding of the pleasures of existence. Perhaps it was that having practiced them all, he no longer found anything unexpected.

He went to the theater, not to follow the show, or glance right and left around the room, but with the sole hope that he would witness a fire. At the fair in Neuilly, he followed all the performances at the zoo with the expectation of disaster: the tamer devoured by his beasts. He had tried the bullfights, but quickly grew displeased, as the killing there took on a look that was too ordered, too natural, and it disgusted him to watch that kind of suffering.

He sought out the horrible and fleeting anguish of the "never before seen". Once he had lived through a fire at the Opéra-Comique and escaped unhurt; another time he had been two steps from the cage of the beasts the day Fred was devoured by his lions. Now he had almost lost interest in the theater and zoo. To those astonished by this apparent change in his tastes, he replied:

"I've seen them already. They can no longer do anything for me."

When he was deprived of those two favorite pleasures — ten years of his life had passed before he achieved their realization — he went into a slump for months, hardly going out, aimless.

But one morning, the walls of Paris were covered with colorful posters. They showed a strange inclined track on a blue background, knotting and unknotting like a ribbon. At the top was a cyclist, a tiny dot, who seemed to be waiting for a signal before he launched into his dizzying plunge.

The same day, in the newspapers, he read the story of an extraordinary feat, which contained the explanation for that strange poster.

The man needed to hurtle down the narrow track at full speed, climb the loop and descend again. During this fantastic feat, for a second the acrobat would find himself with his head down and feet in the air.

The gymnast invited the press to come examine his bicycle, and to turn the machine around as many times as it liked. He had to prove beyond a doubt that the tour was honest, frank and devoid of all subterfuge, based solely on his calculations of extreme precision, his unerring and cold-blooded reason.

As soon as a man's life is at stake, however, even the coldest blood can grow shaky at the slightest thing.

Since the announcement of the show, our maniac had recovered some of his spirit. After attending the first demonstrations, he was convinced he would find a new emotion, and the night the races began, he was the first in place to watch the "buckling of the loop".

He had rented a box seat on the extension of the runway, and in that spot, alone, not wanting anyone near him who might distract his attention, he followed the dizzying jump.

It all lasted barely a few seconds. He had just enough time to see the black spot charge down the whiteness of the track, a tremendous run-up before the dive, a giant leap. He felt an anguish quick as a flash of lightning.

But as he left, mixing with the crowd, he reflected that after maybe two or three times, that sight would become no more than a shiver, and then he would become as indifferent about it as he was to everything else.

He grew annoyed again, thinking: "I'm still not at that point yet!" Then he reflected that the cold blood of a man has limits, that the solidity of a bicycle is not, after all, a decisive thing, and that the track was not so resistant it could not, at some moment, collapse. He arrived at the conclusion that inevitably, an accident would have to occur.

From this conclusion to his decision to wait for the accident was no more than a step.

"I will watch the 'buckling of the loop' every night until this man breaks his face," he decided. "And if that doesn't happen during the three months he spends in Paris, I'll follow him wherever he goes!"

For two months, every evening at the same time, he entered the same box, settled into the same place...

The accident did not occur, and the maniac ended up having to learn control. He had remained in the rented box seat for the whole series of performances, and when he asked himself the reason behind his expensive fantasy, he could not find a convincing answer.

One evening, the acrobat completed his circuit slightly earlier than usual. In the hallway, he saw the maniac and went toward him. Only a brief introduction was needed.

"I know, sir," the gymnast replied. "You're a regular of the house. You come every evening."

The maniac was surprised and said:

"It's true, I am very interested in your activities... But who could have told you?..."

The man smiled:

"Oh! No one. I see you, that's all."

"Now that's a surprise. At such a height... and at such a time... your mind is free enough to consider the spectators in the room?"

"Oh! I don't consider the spectators in the room. That would be far too dangerous, and I need my whole presence of mind far too much to look for faces in the crowd. But in our profession, in its theory and practice, there is a method, a trick..."

The maniac was surprised:

"A trick?"...

"Let's be clear, this is not a fraud. But it's something the public has no idea about, although it is the most delicate part of the exercise. The fact is that it's impossible to empty the brain to the point of not having a single thought, to the point that the will doesn't disperse, so to speak. So, out of all the room, I choose one object, one fixed point where I can fix my gaze. I see nothing but this point, this object. From the second it's in my eyes, nothing else exists. I'm on the saddle. My hands grip the handlebars, and I worry about nothing: not my balance, not my direction. I'm sure of my muscles, solid as steel. There's only one part of myself I must be careful with: My eyes. But once they're attached to something, they no longer make me afraid. The night I started, who knows why, my gaze fell on your box. I've seen you. I've seen nothing but you. Without realizing it, you have taken my eyes... You have been the point, the object of my concentration. The second day I looked for you in the same place. Same thing all the next days. Now, as soon as I enter, by instinct my eyes look for you, they follow you. You are precious, an essential aid to my circuit. Given this, you understand that the least I can do is meet you."

The next day, as usual, the maniac was in his box. There was a movement in the room, a bustling noise. Suddenly a deep silence fell; no breath seemed to come from any chest. The acrobat mounted his bike, held by two men, and waited for the starting signal. He was perfectly level, fists on the handlebars, head facing forward, gaze steady.

He shouted: "Go!" and the men pushed him.

But at the same time, with the most natural movement in the world, the maniac stood up and sat on the other side of his box. A gruesome thing then happened. The acrobat gave a violent jump. His bike, which shot forward, gave a tremendous lurch, leaped off the track and crashed to the ground in the midst of terrified shrieks.

With a businesslike gesture, the maniac put on his overcoat, smoothed his hat with the back of his sleeve and made his exit.

The Father

When the last spadeful of earth had been scooped up and they'd given the last handshake, father and son returned home slowly, in silence, their legs heavy and their heads empty, overcome suddenly by the great weariness that follows efforts sustained for too long.

The house, still filled with the scent of flowers, calm again after the disorder, the comings and goings of the last two days, seemed strangely empty. The old maid who had come back before them had put everything in order, so that it felt like they were returning from a long journey, but without the joy, without that great sigh, saying: "Ah! At last we are at home!…"

Everything was tidy and clean. Beside the fireplace, the cat lay curled up, purring softly, and the gentle cheer of the winter sun could be seen through the windows.

The father sat by the fire, shook his head and sighed:

"Your poor mother!…"

And two tears slid down his good round face, his kind face that grief, the cold of being outside and the warmth of the room had swollen slightly.

Then, needing to hear something besides the purring of the cat, the ticking of the clock and the crackling of logs in the fireplace, seized without his knowing it by the pride of the living when confronted with the departed, he began to speak:

"Did you see the Duponts? They were all there, and the presence of the grandfather moved me very much…

Your mother liked them… But how is it that your friend Brémaud didn't come?… Yes, I know… With so many people, it's possible I didn't notice him…

He sighed again: "My poor little one!…", overcome by a fussing affection for this big twenty-five year old boy who sat beside him, crying silently.

The old maid came in on tiptoe, so quietly they didn't hear the door open.

"Come, sir! We must not go on like this! We must eat!"

They looked up.

It was true! They had to eat. Life swept them up again. They were hungry, not that happy hunger of the old days when they'd loved to sit down comfortably at table, but the hunger of animals when they feel their stomachs empty. So far, modesty had restrained them. Now, they looked at one another without saying anything, both wishing and fearing the first conversation at the overly large table, next to the empty place.

The father, eyes full of tears, murmured:

"Yes, you're right… We must eat… We must, my little one…"

The son nodded and rose:

"I'll go change and come back."

He went out. The door closed, and as he mechanically entered his mother's bedroom, the old maid came up to him, and said in a low voice:

"Mister Jean, I have something for you… a letter your mother entrusted to me, eight days ago, when she knew she was lost… She told me to give it to you… afterward. Here it is."

He paused, surprised, and looked at the maid. There she stood before him, hesitant, the envelope she was holding out to him trembling in her fingers, and all at once he had the sharp feeling that a great pain, a great secret, lay waiting there before him.

He said, with a lump in his throat:

"Give it to me… and go back in."

As soon as he was alone, without thinking, he locked the door with two turns of the key. The room, with its bed that was too flat, its curtains that were drawn too tight, its fireplace without a fire and its furniture too neatly arranged, already had an abandoned look.

Trembling, he turned the letter over and over in his fingers, paralyzed by the sight of that writing of the dead, that dear writing that he had seen so often, that appeared on the slightly crumpled paper now spread before him.

Through the wall, he could hear the maid come and go, setting the table. He tore open the envelope and read:

"My darling son,

I feel the hour of eternal farewell is near. I go without weakness, and almost without regret, since you are a man now and you haven't needed me for a long time. I am conscious of having seemed an impeccable mother. But a very heavy secret rests between us, one that I haven't had the courage to reveal to you, but that it is necessary you know.

Your mother, the one you loved and respected above all, the one to whom you told your troubles when you were small and your sorrows when you were a man, this mother of yours, my dear, is very guilty.

You are not the son of the one you have always called 'Father'. There was in my life a great, an immense love, and my only crime was not to confess. Your father, your true father, is alive. He has watched you grow up from afar, and he loves you, I know it. You are at the age you can make the most serious decisions. Your whole life can be remade again, if you want. You can be rich tomorrow, if you find in yourself the courage I lacked. The act I am committing is cowardly, I know… Since I lived badly, I can only die that way too. A hundred times I was on the verge of fleeing this house, of taking you with me. I didn't have the energy… The smallest thing would have been enough to give it to me: a suspicion… a harsh word… but there was nothing!… not a cloud…"

He paused, crushed by the revelation.

So his mother had taken a lover!… She had been able to bear that secret for so long. She had been able to talk and smile, without a quiver to betray her guilt and remorse! And he, once pitiless before the weaknesses of women, he for whom all pride, all reverence, all joy were summarized in that single word: "Mother!…" had grown up there, a stranger, a living insult to that honest man who had shown him nothing but affection and kindness!…

His whole childhood rose up before him. Once again he saw himself, small, so small, walking through the streets of the city, putting his hand in his father's… He grew older… A very serious illness held him for long months between life and death, and once again he saw his father sitting by his bedside, trying to smile with tears in his eyes… Time passed… Business went badly, and there were other memories, sharp and poignant… conversations he heard in the evening curled up in bed. His mother hardly spoke, while his father said: "I'll cut back… I won't smoke, I'll stop going to the café… My clothes will hold out for a long while… What's most important is that the boy doesn't suffer… It's a bad patch to get through, that's all… By tightening our belts here and there, we can still give him sweets… Little ones have their whole life before them to suffer... What good would grief do to them so early!..."

And that was the man she'd cheated!...

He began to cry. The sentence in her letter came back to him: You are at the age you can make the most serious decisions."

It was true. He didn't even have the right to hesitate.

Not for a second did the idea of wealth cross his mind. He'd simply have the courage that she'd been lacking. He'd leave this house without saying anything... He'd go far, far away, never to return. That way, the shame of knowing would go with him. How could he sit at that table without blushing now? How could he listen to that kind voice saying "My little one" and recalling the memory of "poor Mama"?

He made a decision, sobbing:

"Oh! Mama, Mama! What have you done!..."

Goodbye to the tranquil and calm life, the tender reminiscences of the dead past. He had no right to continue the lie, the mistake. He remained motionless, lost in his sorrow.

A noise came from the dining room.

"... Poor little one!... He's grieving!... He's in his mother's bedroom... Let him cry... Ah! We are very unhappy... I feel so old! At least I still have him! He's a good boy, he won't leave me!"

He raised his head and bit his lips. His father was still speaking, and little by little, listening to him, his thoughts took a different course. The way he had to follow seemed less clear to him, his duty seemed more confused.

"He won't leave me..."

Did he have the right to abandon this poor man, to leave him all alone to get older in this deserted house?... Leave! Was that the way he would repay his affection, his efforts, his sacrifices?...

But he wasn't his son... His presence here, under his roof, was something unbearable, hateful...

He had to decide right away. Later it would be too late. Still holding his mother's letter, he began to read it again:

"The smallest thing would have given me the energy to leave: a suspicion... a harsh word... but there was nothing!... not a cloud..."

His father's voice continued on the other side of the wall:

"Yes, I've lived twenty-seven years with her, and during all that time, nothing, not a cloud..."

The same words... the same sentence!...

He went on reading:

"And now I'll tell you the name of your real father. It is..."

The letter trembled in his fingers. One look, and the name forever would be engraved on his eyes, in his being... and so... so... he could not...

The voice called gently:

"Come, my little one, come to the table..."

Shuddering deeply, he closed his eyes a moment. Then he took a match, raised his hand and set fire to the paper. He watched it burn slowly, and when the flames licked his nails, he opened his fingers. A square of black ash fell to the ground. A white corner, very nearly engulfed... Then nothing...

He pulled open the door, and stood for a moment without moving on the threshold. But when he saw the good man before him with his kind face, red eyes and trembling hands, he took him in his arms, embraced him tightly, as one embraces a loved one thought to have been lost forever, and wept:

"Papa! My dear Papa!…"

SF & FANTASY

Adolphe Alhaiza. *Cybele*

Alphonse Allais. *The Adventures of Captain Cap*

Henri Allorge. *The Great Cataclysm*

Guy d'Armen. *Doc Ardan: The City of Gold and Lepers; The Trog-lodytes of Mount Everest/The Giants of Black Lake; The Abominable Snowman*

G.-J. Arnaud. *The Ice Company*

André Arnyvelde. *The Ark; The Mutilated Bacchus*

Charles Asselineau. *The Double Life*

Henri Austruy. *The Eupantophone; The Olotelepan; The Petitpaon Era*

Barillet-Lagargousse. *The Final War*

Cyprien Bérard. *The Vampire Lord Ruthwen*

S. Henry Berthoud. *Martyrs of Science*

Aloysius Bertrand. *Gaspard de la Nuit*

Richard Bessière. *The Gardens of the Apocalypse; The Masters of Silence*

Chevalier de Béthune. *The World of Mercury*

Albert Bleunard. *Ever Smaller*

Félix Bodin. *The Novel of the Future*

Pierre Boitard. *Journey to the Sun*

Louis Boussenard. *Monsieur Synthesis*

Alphonse Brown. *City of Glass; The Conquest of the Air*

Émile Calvet. *In a Thousand Years*

André Caroff. *The Terror of Madame Atomos; Miss Atomos; The Return of Madame Atomos; The Mistake of Madame Atomos; The Monsters of Madame Atomos; The Revenge of Madame Atomos; The Resurrection of Madame Atomos; The Mark of Madame Atomos; The Spheres of Madame Atomos; The Wrath of Madame Atomos* (w/M. & Sylvie Stéphan)

Félicien Champsaur. *Homo-Deus; The Human Arrow; Nora, The Ape-Woman; Ouha, King of the Apes; Pharaoh's Wife*

Didier de Chousy. *Ignis*

Jules Clarétie. *Obsession*

Jacques Collin de Plancy. *Voyage to the Center of the Earth*

Michel Corday. *The Eternal Flame; The Lynx* (w/André Couvreur)

André Couvreur. *Caresco, Superman; The Exploits of Professor Tornada* (3 vols.); *The Necessary Evil*

Gaston Danville. *The Perfume of Lust*
Camille Debans. *The Misfortunes of John Bull*
Captain Danrit. *Undersea Odyssey*
C. I. Defontenay. *Star (Psi Cassiopeia)*
Charles Derennes. *The People of the Pole*
Georges Dodds (anthologist). *The Missing Link*
Charles Dodeman. *The Silent Bomb*
Harry Dickson. *The Heir of Dracula; Harry Dickson vs. The Spider*
Jules Dornay. *Lord Ruthven Begins*
Alfred Driou. *The Adventures of a Parisian Aeronaut*
Odette Dulac. *The War of the Sexes*
Alexandre Dumas. *The Return of Lord Ruthven*
Renée Dunan. *Baal; The Ultimate Pleasure*
J.-C. Dunyach. *The Night Orchid; The Thieves of Silence*
Henri Duvernois. *The Man Who Found Himself*
Achille Eyraud. *Voyage to Venus*
Henri Falk. *The Age of Lead*
Paul Féval. *Anne of the Isles; Knightshade; Revenants; Vampire City; The Vampire Countess; The Wandering Jew's Daughter*
Paul Féval, *fils. Felifax, the Tiger-Man*
Charles de Fieux. *Lamékis*
Fernand Fleuret. *Jim Click*
Charles-Marie Flor O'Squarr. *Phantoms*
Louis Forest. *Someone is Stealing Children in Paris*
Arnould Galopin. *Doctor Omega; Doctor Omega and the Shadowmen* (anthology)
Judith Gautier. *Isoline and the Serpent-Flower*
H. Gayar. *The Marvelous Adventures of Serge Myrandhal on Mars*
Louis Geoffroy. *The Apocryphal Napoleon*
G.L. Gick. *Harry Dickson and the Werewolf of Rutherford Grange*
Raoul Gineste. *The Second Life of Doctor Albin*
Delphine de Girardin. *Balzac's Cane*
Léon Gozlan. *The Vampire of the Val-de-Grâce*
Jules Gros. *The Fossil Man*
Jimmy Guieu. *The Polarian-Denebian War* (2 vols.)
Edmond Haraucourt. *Daah, the First Human; Illusions of Immortality*
Nathalie Henneberg. *The Green Gods*
Eugène Hennebert. *The Enchanted City*
Jules Hoche. *The Maker of Men and His Formula*
V. Hugo, P. Foucher & P. Meurice. *The Hunchback of Notre-Dame*
Romain d'Huissier. *Hexagon: Dark Matter*

Jules Janin. *The Magnetized Corpse*

Michel Jeury. *Chronolysis*

Gustave Kahn. *The Tale of Gold and Silence*

Gérard Klein. *The Mote in Time's Eye*

Fernand Kolney. *Love in 5000 Years*

Paul Lacroix. *Danse Macabre*

Louis-Guillaume de La Follie. *The Unpretentious Philosopher*

Jean de La Hire. *The Fiery Wheel; Enter the Nyctalope; The Nyctalope on Mars; The Nyctalope vs. Lucifer; The Nyctalope Steps In; Night of the Nyctalope; Return of the Nyctalope*

Etienne-Léon de Lamothe-Langon. *The Virgin Vampire*

André Laurie. *Spiridon*

Gabriel de Lautrec. *The Vengeance of the Oval Portrait*

Alain le Drimeur. *The Future City*

Georges Le Faure & Henri de Graffigny. *The Extraordinary Adventures of a Russian Scientist Across the Solar System* (2 vols.)

Gustave Le Rouge. *The Dominion of the World* (w/Gustave Guitton) (4 vols.); *The Mysterious Doctor Cornelius* (3 vols.); *The Vampires of Mars*

Jules Lermina. *The Battle of Strasbourg; Mysteryville; Panic in Paris; The Secret of Zippelius; To-Ho and the Gold Destroyers*

André Lichtenberger. *The Centaurs; The Children of the Crab*

Maurice Limat. *Mephista*

Listonai. *The Philosophical Voyager*

Jean-Marc & Randy Lofficier. *Edgar Allan Poe on Mars; The Katrina Protocol; Pacifica 1, 2; Robonocchio; Return of the Nyctalope;* (anthologists) *Tales of the Shadowmen 1-13; The Vampire Almanac* (2 vols.)

Ch. Lomon & P.-B. Gheuzi. *The Last Days of Atlantis*

Camille Mauclair. *The Virgin Orient*

Xavier Mauméjean. *The League of Heroes*

Joseph Méry. *The Tower of Destiny*

Hippolyte Mettais. *Paris Before the Deluge; The Year 5865*

Louise Michel. *The Human Microbes; The New World*

Tony Moilin. *Paris in the Year 2000*

José Moselli. *Illa's End*

John-Antoine Nau. *Enemy Force*

Marie Nizet. *Captain Vampire*

Charles Nodier. *Trilby and The Crumb Fairy*

C. Nodier, A. Beraud & Toussaint-Merle. *Frankenstein*

Henri de Parville. *An Inhabitant of the Planet Mars*

Gaston de Pawlowski. *Journey to the Land of the 4th Dimension*
Georges Pellerin. *The World in 2000 Years*
Ernest Pérochon. *The Frenetic People*
Pierre Pelot. *The Child Who Walked on the Sky*
Jean Petithuguenin. *An International Mission to the Moon*
J. Polidori, C. Nodier, E. Scribe. *Lord Ruthven the Vampire*
P.-A. Ponson du Terrail. *The Immortal Woman; The Vampire and the Devil's Son*
Georges Price. *The Missing Men of the* Sirius
René Pujol. *The Chimerical Quest*
Edgar Quinet. *Ahasuerus; The Enchanter Merlin*
Henri de Régnier. *A Surfeit of Mirrors*
Maurice Renard. *The Blue Peril; Doctor Lerne; The Doctored Man; A Man Among the Microbes; The Master of Light*
Restif de la Bretonne. *The Discovery of the Austral Continent by a Flying Man; Posthumous Correspondence* (3 vols.)
Jean Richepin. *The Crazy Corner; The Wing*
Albert Robida. *The Adventures of Saturnin Farandoul; Chalet in the Sky; The Clock of the Centuries; The Electric Life; The Engineer Von Satanas*
J.-H. Rosny Aîné. *Helgvor of the Blue River; The Givreuse Enigma; The Mysterious Force; The Navigators of Space; Vamireh; The World of the Variants; The Young Vampire*
Marcel Rouff. *Journey to the Inverted World*
Marie-Anne de Roumier-Robert. *The Voyage of Lord Seaton to the Seven Planets*
Léonie Rouzade. *The World Turned Upside Down*
Han Ryner. *The Human Ant; The Superhumans*
Louis-Claude de Saint-Martin. *The Crocodile*
Frank Schildiner. *The Quest of Frankenstein*
Pierre de Selenes: *An Unknown World*
Norbert Sevestre. *Sâr Dubnotal: Vs. Jack the Ripper; The Astral Trail*
Angelo de Sorr. *The Vampires of London*
Brian Stableford. *The Empire of the Necromancers (1. The Shadow of Frankenstein; 2. Frankenstein and the Vampire Countess; 3. Frankenstein in London); The Wayward Muse; Eurydice's Lament; The Mirror of Dionysius; The New Faust at the Tragicomique; Sherlock Holmes and The Vampires of Eternity; The Stones of Camelot* (anthologist) *News from the Moon; The Germans on Venus; The Supreme Progress; The World Above the World; Nemoville; Investiga-*

tions of the Future; The Conqueror of Death; The Revolt of the Ma-chines; The Man With the Blue Face; The Aerial Valley; The New Moon; The Nickel Man; On the Brink of the World's End; The Mirror of Present Events; The Humanishere
Jacques Spitz. *The Eye of Purgatory*
Kurt Steiner. *Ortog*
Eugène Thébault. *Radio-Terror*
C.-F. Tiphaigne de La Roche. *Amilec*
Simon Tyssot de Patot. *The Strange Voyages of Jacques Massé and Pierre de Mésange*
Louis Ulbach. *Prince Bonifacio*
Théo Varlet. *The Castaways of Eros; The Golden Rock.; The Martian Epic* (w/Octave Joncquel); *Timeslip Troopers* (w/André Blandin); *The Xenobiotic Invasion*
Pierre Véron. *The Merchants of Health*
Paul Vibert. *The Mysterious Fluid*
Villiers de l'Isle-Adam. *The Scaffold; The Vampire Soul*
Gaston de Wailly. *The Murderer of the World*
Philippe Ward. *Artahe; Manhattan Ghost* (w/Mickael Laguerre); *The Song of Montségur* (w/Sylvie Miller)

Victor Margueritte. *The Bacheloress; The Companion; The Couple*

MYSTERIES & THRILLERS

M. Allain & P. Souvestre. *The Daughter of Fantômas*
A. Anicet-Bourgeois & Lucien Dabril. *Rocambole* (stage plays)
Guy d'Armen. *Doc Ardan: The City of Gold and Lepers; The Trog-lodytes of Mount Everest/The Giants of Black Lake; Doc Ardan: The Abominable Snowman*
Cyprien Bérard. *The Vampire Lord Ruthwen*
A. Bernède. *Belphegor; Judex* (w/Louis Feuillade); *The Return of Judex* (w/Louis Feuillade); *The Shadow of Judex* (anthology)
A. Bisson & G. Livet. *Nick Carter vs. Fantômas* (stage play)
André Caroff. *The Terror of Madame Atomos; Miss Atomos; The Return of Madame Atomos; The Mistake of Madame Atomos; The Monsters of Madame Atomos; The Revenge of Madame Atomos; The Resurrection of Madame Atomos; The Mark of Madame Atomos; The Spheres of Madame Atomos; The Wrath of Madame Atomos* (w/M. & Sylvie Stéphan)

Félicien Champsaur. *Homo-Deus; Nora, The Ape-Woman; Ouha, King of the Apes*

Jules Clarétie. *Obsession*

V. Darlay & H. de Gorsse. *Arsène Lupin vs. Sherlock Holmes: The Stage Play* (stage play)

Harry Dickson. *Harry Dickson vs. The Heir of Dracula; Harry Dickson vs. The Spider*

Séamas Duffy. *Sherlock Holmes in Paris*

Alexandre Dumas. *The Return of Lord Ruthven* (stage play)

Paul Féval. *The Black Coats (The Parisian Jungle; Heart of Steel; The Sword-Swallower; 'Salem Street; The Invisible Weapon; The Companions of the Treasure; The Cadet Gang); Gentlemen of the Night; John Devil*

Paul Féval, *fils. Felifax, the Tiger-Man*

Louis Forest. *Someone is Stealing Children in Paris*

Émile Gaboriau. *Monsieur Lecoq; The Casebook of Monsieur Lecoq*

Arnould Galopin: *Harry Dickson: The Man in Grey; Harry Dickson: Tenebras*

Goron & Émile Gautier. *Spawn of the Penitentiary*

G.L. Gick. *Harry Dickson and The Werewolf of Rutherford Grange*

Léon Gozlan. *The Vampire of the Val-de-Grâce*

Georges Grison. *The Heads that fell in Paris*

Paul d'Ivoi. *Around the World on Five Sous* (w/Henri Chabrillat)

Paul Lacroix. *Danse Macabre*

Jean de La Hire. *Enter the Nyctalope; The Nyctalope on Mars; The Nyctalope vs. Lucifer; The Nyctalope Steps In; Night of the Nyctalope; Return of the Nyctalope*

Rick Lai. *Shadows of the Opera: Retribution in Blood; Sisters of the Shadows: The Curse of Cagliostro*

Etienne-Léon de Lamothe-Langon. *The Virgin Vampire*

Steve Leadley. *Sherlock Holmes and The Circle of Blood*

Maurice Leblanc. *Arsène Lupin vs. Countess Cagliostro; Arsène Lupin vs. Sherlock Holmes (1. The Blonde Phantom; 2. The Hollow Needle); The Island of the Thirty Coffin; 813; The Many Faces of Arsène Lupin* (anthology)

Gustave Lerouge: *The Mysterious Doctor Cornelius* (3 vols.)

Gaston Leroux. *Chéri-Bibi* (stage play); *The Phantom of the Opera; Rouletabille & the Mystery of the Yellow Room; Rouletabille at Krupp's*

Maurice Limat. *Mephista*

Jean-Marc & Randy Lofficier. *The Katrina Protocol;* (anthologists) *Tales of the Shadowmen 1-13; The Vampire Almanac* (2 vols.)

Richard Marsh. *The Complete Adventures of Judith Lee*

William Patrick Maynard. *The Terror of Fu Manchu; The Destiny of Fu Manchu*

Frank J. Morlok. *Sherlock Holmes: The Grand Horizontals* (stage play)*; Sherlock Holmes vs Jack the Ripper* (stage pla*y); Sherlock Holmes, Fantômas, Lupin, Raffles and More: The Spanish Plays* (stage plays)

Jean Petithuguenin. *The Adventures of Ethel King, The Female Nick Carter*

P.-A. Ponson du Terrail. *The Immortal Woman; The Vampire and the Devil's Son*

Georges Price. *The Missing Men of the* Sirius

Charles Rabou: *The Secret Bureau 1; The secret Bureau 2: The Brothers of Death*

Antonin Reschal. *The Adventures of Miss Boston, The First Female Detective*

Norbert Sevestre. *Sâr Dubnotal vs. Jack the Ripper; The Astral Trail*

Eugène Thébault. *Radio-Terror*

P. de Wattyne & Y. Walter. *Sherlock Holmes vs. Fantômas* (stage play)

David White. *Fantômas in America*

Pierre Yrondy. *The Adventures of Thérèse Arnaud of the French Secret Service*

NON-FICTION

Stephen R. Bissette. *Blur 1-5. Green Mountain Cinema 1; Teen Angels*

Win Scott Eckert. *Crossovers* (2 vols.)

Georges Grison. *The Heads that Fell in Paris*

Jean-Marc & Randy Lofficier. *Shadowmen* (2 vols.)

Randy Lofficier. *Over Here*

Brian Stableford. *The Plurality of Imaginary Worlds*